LITTLE FADETTE

LITTLE FADETTE

GEORGE SAND

Translated by J.M. Lancaster
Edited by David Allen

HAWTHORNE
CLASSICS

ISBN: 978-1-0879-0832-8

First published in The United States of America

Contents

Preface

After the terrible days of June 1848 were at an end, I withdrew from the world—agitated to the very depths of my soul by the scenes of violence through which we had passed, and hoping to regain in solitude, at least my faith, if not my peace of mind.

If I claimed to be a philosopher, I might believe or pretend to believe, that faith in ideas enables the mind to maintain its serenity amid the deplorable events of contemporaneous history.

But I make no such pretensions. I humbly acknowledge that the conviction that Providence has a future in store for us would have no power to sustain the soul of an artist through the trials of a present fraught with gloom and convulsed by civil war. Men who enter the fray—who take an active part in politics—must, whatever may be the circumstances, be prey to alternate hope and despair, rage and exultation—the elation of triumph or the exasperation of defeat.

But for the poor poet as for the woman who sits, an idle spectator of events—having no direct or personal part in them—there is, whatever may be the outcome of the struggle, a profound abhorrence of bloodshed on either side, grief and despair at beholding the hatred, the insults, the threats, the calumnies which ascend to heaven, like a foul holocaust, in the train of social upheavals.

At such moments as these, a genius like Dante's, impetuous and indomitable, writes with his tears, his nerves at their utmost tension, dipping his pen in gall—a terrible poem, a drama, filled with groans and torture. One's soul must, like his, have been tempered by fire and sword, before one's imagination could conceive the horrors of a symbolic Inferno, when the wretched Purgatory of actual earthly desolation is staring him in the face.

The artist of our less virile and more sensitive age—who is the reflection and echo of his generation —can not resist the impulse to avert his gaze and distract his imagination by turning toward an ideal state of peace and calm contemplation. He need not blush for the weakness to which he yields, for it is also his duty. At a time when such evils arise from men's hatred of each other and lack of mutual understanding, the artist's mission is to extol moderation, mutual confidence, and friendship, and thereby to remind poor, callous, or disheartened humanity, that purity of morals, tender sentiments, and primitive justice still exist or can exist in this world.

Direct allusions to present ills, appeals to excited passions—these do not lead to salvation. A sweet song, an air on the rustic pipe, a tale with which to lull the little ones to sleep—secure and free from pain—is worth far more than the portrayal of real evils, whose colours are deepened and intensified by the power of fiction.

To preach peace and harmony to men engaged in cutting each other's throats is like a voice crying in the wilderness. There are times when men's souls are so disturbed that they are deaf to any direct appeal. Since those June days, of which present events are the inevitable consequence, the author of the tale which you are about to read has assumed the task of being amiable, even if he should die of chagrin. He has allowed them to ridicule his pastoral sketches, just as they have ridiculed everything else, but has not troubled himself as to the decisions of dogmatic criticism. He knows that he has given pleasure to those who love that strain, and that to give pleasure to such as suffer from the same malady as himself—a horror of hatred and the vengeance which follows in its footsteps—is to do them all the good which they are capable of accepting. A brief enjoyment, it is true—a fleeting consolation—but more genuine than the tirades of passion and more impressive than a classic presentation of logical facts.

GEORGE SAND

NOHANT, *December 21, 1851*

I

Chapter 1

Father Barbeau was a member of the municipal council of his commune, so you may take it for granted that he was a man in pretty comfortable circumstances. He had two fields which furnished support for his family and gave him a profit besides. His meadows yielded an abundant crop of hay, and, except for that growing along the brook—which was of rather poor quality on account of the rushes—it was considered the best forage in the neighbourhood. Father Barbeau's house was well built, roofed with tiles, and pleasantly situated on a hillside, with a productive garden and a vineyard of about five acres. Then he had a fine orchard behind his barn—what is called an *ouche* in our part of the country, which bore plenty of fruit—plums, cherries, pears, and sorb apples; and there were no walnut trees, within a couple of leagues, so large and old as those which bordered his land. Father Barbeau was a good, cheerful, simple-hearted man, very devoted to his family, without neglecting the interests of his neighbours and fellow parishioners.

He was already the father of three children, when Mother Barbeau—being no doubt of the opinion that they were able to support five, and that she had better hurry up as she was getting on in years—saw fit to present him with two fine boys at once. As they were so much alike that it was difficult to tell them apart, it was at once evident that they were *bessons*, that is to say, twins who bear a remarkable resemblance to each other. Mother Sagette, who received them in her apron as soon as they came into the world, did not forget to make a little cross with her needle on the arm of the first-born, because, said she, "there might be some mistake about a bit of ribbon or a necklace, and so the child might forfeit his birthright."

"When the child is better able to bear it," said she, "we must make a mark which will last," and this was accordingly done. The elder was named Sylvain, which was soon changed to Sylvinet, to distinguish him from his elder brother, who was his godfather; the younger was called Landry, and kept the name as he had received it at baptism, his uncle, who was his sponsor, being still known as Landriche—the name he had borne as a child.

When Father Barbeau returned from the market, he was rather surprised to see two little heads in the cradle.

"Oh, ho!" said he, "that cradle is too small—I must make it larger tomorrow." He was something of a carpenter, though he had never learned the trade, and had made half his furniture himself. He had nothing further to say on the subject, but set about caring for his wife, who drank a large glass of warm wine, and was all the better for it.

"You are so very industrious, wife, that I ought to feel encouraged to do my part. Here are two more children to feed, though we were not actually in need of them; that means that I must keep on cultivating our land and raising our cattle. Don't fret! I'll work; but see that you don't give me three the next time, for that would be too many."

Mother Barbeau began to cry, which greatly distressed Father Barbeau." There, there, wife!" said he, "you must not worry. I did not say that to distress you, but, on the contrary, by way of thanks. These children are handsome and well-formed—they haven't a blemish about them, and I am quite proud of them."

"Oh, dear me!" said his wife, "I know you don't mean to blame me, master; but I can't help worrying, for I have been told that there is nothing more difficult or risky than bringing up twins. They are a drawback to each other, and it generally turns out that one has to die so that the other may thrive."

"Indeed! " said the father. "Is that true? I don't remember ever to have seen twins before. They don't come often. But here is Mother Sagette, who has had plenty of experience, and will tell us all about it."

So when they appealed to Mother Sagette, she answered: "Just mark my words, these twins will live and thrive, and will have just as good health as other children. I have been a nurse this fifty years, and have seen all the children in the Canton, born, grow up, or die. Twins are no new thing to me. In the first place, it doesn't matter about their looking alike. Sometimes they are no more alike than you and I, and yet one will be strong and the other sickly; so one lives and the other dies. But just look at yours; each one of them is as handsome and well-formed as if he were an only son. They certainly did each other no harm before they came into the world, and they were born without causing their mother too much suffering, and seem to be all right themselves. They are as pretty as pictures and ask nothing better than to be allowed to live. Come, cheer up, Mother Barbeau! You will take great comfort in seeing them grow up, and if they keep on as they have begun, very few people, excepting yourselves and those who see them every day, will be able to know them apart, for I never saw twins so much alike. They are like two little partridges out of the same egg. They are so pretty and so much alike that only the mother bird can know which is which."

"All right," said Father Barbeau, scratching his head; "but I have heard say that twins are so fond of each other that they cannot live apart and that if you separate them, one or the other will grieve itself to death."

"That is perfectly true," said Mother Sagette; "but now, listen to the advice of a woman with experience. Do not forget what I tell you; for perhaps by the time your children are old enough to leave you, I may no longer be living. Take care as soon as your twins are old enough to recognize each other, and don't let them be always together. Take one out to work with you, while the other stays at home. When one goes fishing, send the other out hunting. When one is tending the sheep, let the other go and see to the cattle in the pasture. When you give one a glass of wine, give the other some water, and *vice versa*. Don't scold or correct them both at the same time; don't dress them alike; when one has a hat let the other have a cap, and above all, don't let their blouses be of the same shade of blue. In fact, do everything you can to prevent their being mistaken for each other, and passing themselves off for each other. I am very much afraid that what I am telling you will go in one ear and out of the other, but if you don't follow my advice, you will live to regret it."

Mother Sagette spoke sensibly, and they believed her. They promised her to do as she said, and made her a handsome present before she left. Then, as she had expressly recommended that the twins should not be brought up on the same milk, they at once set about finding a nurse. But there was none to be found in the place. Mother Barbeau, who had not been on the lookout for two children, and who had nursed all the others herself, had not made any arrangements in advance. Father Barbeau was obliged to go about the neighbourhood in search of a nurse, and meanwhile, as the mother could not see her little ones suffer, she suckled them herself.

People in our part of the country take some time making up their minds, and even if they are very well-to-do, must always try to bargain a little. The Barbeaus had the reputation of having considerable property, and it was supposed that as the mother was not as young as she had been, she would not be able to nurse both her children. So all the nurses Father Barbeau could find, asked him eighteen francs a month—just the same as they would charge a bourgeois. Father Barbeau had not expected to give more than twelve or fifteen francs, as he thought that was a good deal for a peasant. He inquired everywhere, and talked the matter over, but without coming to any decision. There was no particular hurry; for two such small children could not exhaust the mother, and they were so healthy, so quiet, and cried so little, that they made scarcely any more trouble in the house than one baby.

They both went to sleep at the same time. The father had en-larged the cradle, and when the children both cried at once, the same rocking soothed them both.

Finally, Father Barbeau engaged a nurse at fifteen francs, and he was only haggling over a gratuity of a hundred sous when his wife said to him: "Pooh, master, I don't see why we should spend a hundred and eighty or two hundred francs a year as if we were ladies and gentlemen, or as if I were too old to nurse my own children. I have more than enough milk for them both. Our boys are nearly a month old, and just see how healthy they are! La Merlaude, whom you are thinking of engaging as a nurse for one of them, is not so strong nor so healthy as I am; her milk is al-ready eighteen months old, and that is not what so young a child needs. La Sagette told us we must not bring up our children on the same milk, so as to prevent their becoming too fond of each other. But didn't she say, too, that we must take as good care of one as of the other? After all, twins are not so hardy as other children. I would rather that our boys should love each other too dearly than that one should be sacrificed for the other. I may say that I have been very fond of all my children, but, somehow or other, these seem to me to be the prettiest little darlings I have ever held in my arms. I have a queer feeling about them, which makes me always feel afraid that I may lose them. Give up thinking of engaging a nurse, husband—please do! In every other respect, we will follow Mother Sagette's advice. How can two children still at the breast grow too fond of each other, I should like to know when they will hardly be able to tell their hands from their feet when they are old enough to be weaned?"

"What you say is very true, wife," answered Father Barbeau,

looking at his wife, who was still fresher and stronger than most women; "but what should we do if your health should fail as the children grow bigger?"

"Never fear," said Mother Barbeau; " my appetite is as good as when I was fifteen, and besides, if I find that I am running down, I promise you that I will let you know, and there will still be time to send one of these poor children out to nurse."

Father Barbeau agreed, the more readily as he was not much inclined to incur any unnecessary expense. Mother Barbeau nursed her twins uncomplainingly and was none the worse for it, and she had such a fine constitution that, two years after weaning her little ones, she gave birth to a pretty little girl named Nanette, which she also nursed herself. But it was a little too much for her, and she could hardly have managed it, if her eldest daughter, who had just had her first child, had not come to her assistance by occasionally nursing her little sister. And so the whole family grew up and were soon swarming about in the sunshine—the little uncles and aunts with the little nephews and nieces, none of whom could lay claim to being any better or any worse than the others.

II

Chapter 2

The twins grew apace and were not ill any oftener than other children, and they were so good-tempered and amiable that it really seemed as if they did not suffer as much in teething and growing as the rest of the little ones. They were blond and continued blond all their lives. They were very good-looking, with large blue eyes, fine sloping shoulders, straight, well-formed bodies—larger and stronger than other children of their age, and all the people from the neighbourhood who passed through La Cosse stopped to take a look at them and to wonder at their resemblance to each other, and everybody went off saying, "That is certainly a fine pair of boys!" In this way, the twins became early accustomed to being inspected and questioned, so that they did not grow up bashful and silly. They were quite at their ease with everybody, and instead of hiding behind the bushes as country children do whenever they see a stranger, they spoke to everybody who came along, but always very politely and answered any questions without hanging their heads or waiting to be asked twice. At first sight, there seemed to be no difference between them, and they were thought to be as much alike as two peas. But after looking at them for a few minutes, you could see that Landry was a shade taller and stronger, that his hair was a little thicker, his nose more prominent, and his eyes brighter. His forehead was broader too, and he looked more determined, and while his brother had a mark on his left cheek, he had a similar one on his right cheek, only much more distinct. The people of the district could distinguish them readily enough, but they had to look closely, and at nightfall or at a little distance, almost everybody confused them, particularly as their voices were very much alike, and as, knowing how easy it was to mistake one for the other, they answered to each other's names without troubling themselves to correct the error. Even Father Barbeau was sometimes confused, but, as Sagette had prophesied, their mother alone never made a mistake, whether they were in the dark or at so great distance off that she could just see them coming or hear their voices.

In fact, there was nothing to choose between them, and if Landry was a trifle gayer and more high-spirited than his brother, Sylvinet was so affectionate and intelligent that he was quite as lovable as his younger brother. For the first three months, their parents tried to prevent their growing fond of each other. Three months is a long time for country people to continue doing anything to which they are unaccustomed. But, on the one hand, they could not see that it made any difference, and on the other, M. le Curd had told them that Mother Sagette was in her dotage and that what the dear Lord had ordained by natural law, could not be undone by man. So that by and by they forgot what they had promised to do. The first time the little boys left off their frocks to go to mass in trousers, they were dressed in the same cloth, for both suits were made out of a petticoat of their mother's, and were just alike, for the parish tailor did not know how to make them any other way. As they grew older, it was noticed that they liked the same colours, and when their Aunt Rosette wished to make them a present of a cravat on New Year's Day, they both chose one of the same shade of lilac, out of the pack of the pedlar who carried his merchandise from door to door on the back of his Percheron horse. Their aunt asked them if it was because they wanted to be dressed alike, but the twins did not think that far. Sylvinet answered that the pedlar had not another cravat in his stock so pretty in colour and design, and Landry at once agreed that all the other cravats were ugly.

"And how do you like the colour of my horse?" asked the pedlar, laughing.

"It is very ugly," said Landry. "It looks like an old magpie."

"Just as ugly as can be," said Sylvinet. "It looks like a half-fledged magpie."

"You see," said the pedlar to their aunt, looking very wise, "that these children see everything the same. If one sees yellow where he ought to see red, the other will as quickly see red where he ought to see yellow, and it is of no use arguing the matter with them; for they say when you try to prevent twins from regarding themselves as cast in the same die, they become idiots and can't tell what they are talking about."

The pedlar said this because his lilac cravats were not fast colour, and he was anxious to find a customer who would take two of them.

As time went on, all this continued, and the twins were dressed so exactly alike that people confused them still more frequently, and whether from a spirit of childish mischief or in accordance with that natural law which the cure believed it impossible to set aside, when one had broken the toe of his sabot, the other soon chipped a piece off of his, for the corresponding foot. When one tore his jacket or his cap, the other never rested till he had imitated the tear so perfectly that it was impossible to tell that it was not caused by the same accident; and then the twins would begin to laugh, and put on an air of lamblike innocence when they were questioned about it.

For weal or woe, this affection increased with age, and by the time they could use their reason a little, the children made up their minds that neither of them could play with other children when his twin brother was absent. Once when their father tried keeping one of them with him all day, while the other stayed at home with his mother, they both were so sad, so pale, and worked with so little spirit, that the parents thought they must be ill. And then, when they met again in the evening, they wandered off together, hand in hand, and did not want to come in, because they were so glad to see each other again, and also because they were a little put out with their parents for making them so uncomfortable. This experiment was not repeated; for, to tell the truth, father and mother, sisters and brothers, uncles and aunts, were so fond of the twins that they were inclined to spoil them. They took great pride in them because they received so many compliments and also because they were neither ugly, silly, nor naughty.

Once in awhile Father Barbeau would worry a little as to what was to be the result of this habit of being always together, after they should grow to be men, and recalling La Sagette's words, he tried to make them jealous of each other by teasing them. For instance, if they played some prank, he would pull Sylvinet's ears, saying to Landry, "I'll forgive you this time, for you generally behave better than your brother." But Sylvinet soon forgot his tingling ears—he was so pleased that Landry had escaped punishment. They also tried giving to one what both wanted; but, if it was something to eat, they divided it between them, or if it happened to be a toy or a little tool, they made common property of it or handed it back and forth without question of ownership. If one was praised for his good conduct, with apparent injustice to the other, that other was proud and pleased to see his twin petted and encouraged, and began to flatter him too. In short, it was useless attempting to separate them in mind or body, and as we none of us like to vex children whom we love, even when it is for their good, they soon let things take their own course, or rather they turned their little teasings into a game which did not deceive the children. They were very sharp-witted and they sometimes pretended to quarrel and fight so that they might be let alone; but they were only in fun, and took care not to hurt each other even the least little bit in the world, as they rolled over and over on the ground. If some passer-by was astonished to see them squabbling, they would hide themselves and laugh at him, and before long you would hear them chattering and twittering away like two blackbirds on one branch.

In spite of this devoted affection and this close resemblance, God, who has made no two things precisely alike in heaven or earth, ordained that their fates should be very unlike, and so it became evident that He intended them to be two distinct beings—quite dissimilar in temperament.

It was not till after they had made their first communion together, that something occurred which showed this to be the case. Father Barbeau's family was on the increase, thanks to his two elder daughters, who had given birth to a goodly number of handsome children. His eldest son, Martin—a fine, handsome fellow—was out at service; his sons-in-law were all industrious men, but work was often scarce. We have had a succession of bad years in our part of the country—as much from severe storms as from business troubles—which have robbed the country people's pockets of more crowns than they put into them. So Father Barbeau did not feel able to keep his whole family at home, and he began to think that it was time to put his twins out at work. Father Caillaud de la Priche offered to take one of them to drive his oxen; for he had a large farm to cultivate, and all his own boys were too big or too little for that work. Mother Barbeau was both alarmed and distressed when her husband first spoke to her about it. She had worried about this very thing all their lives, and yet she felt as if it was the first time the subject had been mentioned; but as she was a very obedient and submissive wife, she had nothing to say. The father also felt anxious and had made all his arrangements in advance. At first, the twins cried, and spent three days wandering about the woods and meadows, and were never seen except at meal-times. They would not say a word to their parents, and when they were asked if they had made up their minds to consent, they did not answer but talked it over a good deal when they were alone together.

The first day they could do nothing but grieve over the approaching separation and walked about arm in arm as if they feared that their parents might resort to force. Father Barbeau, however, would never have done that. He had all a peasant's shrewdness, which is half patience and half trust in the magical effect of time. So the next day the twins, seeing that nobody was going to scold them and that their parents relied upon their good sense to bring them to reason, were more afraid of offending their father than they would have been if he had threatened to punish them.

"We'll have to make up our minds to submit," said Landry, "and the thing is, to decide which of us is to go; for they have left it to us, and Father Caillaud says that he cannot take us both."

"What difference does it make to me whether I go or stay," said Sylvinet, "when you are going to leave us? It is not only the fact of going to live somewhere else that I am thinking about—if you were going with me I should soon feel at home there."

"It is easy enough to say that," answered Landry, "and still the one who stays at home will have more to comfort him, and will not have so many things to worry about as the one who will have to part from his twin brother, his father, his mother, his garden, his animals, and everything which gives him any pleasure."

Landry spoke with considerable firmness, but Sylvinet began to cry again; for he was not so plucky as his brother, and the idea of giving up everything at once made him so unhappy that he could no longer restrain his tears.

Landry cried, too, but not so much and not in the same way;

for he was always thinking of taking the greater share of the trouble on his own shoulders, and he wanted to see how much his brother could bear so that he might spare him the rest. He knew that Sylvinet hated more than he to live in a strange place, and with people who were not his relatives.

"See here, brother," said he, "if we can make up our minds to live apart, I would better be the one to go. I am a little stronger than you, you know, and when we are ill—which almost always happens at the same time—your fever is always higher than mine. They say that perhaps we'll die if we are separated; I don't believe that I shall die, but I cannot answer for you, and that is why I should rather leave you with our mother, who will comfort you and take care of you. To tell the truth, if there is any difference made between us—and I hardly think there is—I believe you are the favourite, and I know you are the most winning and affectionate. So you must stay and I will go. We shall not be far away from each other. Father Caillaud's land is next to ours, and we shall see each other every day. I like to work and it will keep me from thinking too much about you, and as I am a faster runner than you, it will not take me so long to come over and see you as soon as my day's work is done. You will not have much to do and can walk over to see me at work. I shall be much easier about you than if you were away and I at home. So I hope you will stay."

III

Chapter 3

But Sylvinet would not listen to that. Though he was more devoted to his father and mother and little Nanette than Landry
was, he shrank from allowing his beloved twin to bear the whole
burden. After talking it over, they drew straws, and the lot fell
on Landry. This did not satisfy Sylvinet, and he insisted on tossing up a penny. Three times it fell face up for him, and it was
always Landry's lot to go.

"You see it is my fate," said Landry, "and it is of no use to
fight against it." The third day, Sylvinet had not done crying, but
Landry hardly shed a tear. The idea of going away had perhaps,
at first, been more distressing to him than to his brother, because he was fully aware of the demands it would make on his
courage, and also realized how impossible it would be to resist
his parents' wishes. But he had grown accustomed to his trouble
by thinking it over and had reasoned with himself a good deal,

whereas Sylvinet had given way to his feelings to such an extent that he was no longer able to take the matter into calm consideration, and Landry had quite decided to go before Sylvinet had made up his mind to consent to his going.

Then Landry had rather more self-esteem than his brother. They had been so often told that they would never be more than half men if they did not get used to being separated, that Landry, who began to feel the pride of his fourteen years, wanted to show them that he was no longer a child. He had always had great influence over his brother, from the time when they first climbed to the tops of the trees after bird's nests, down to the present day. So now, he succeeded in pacifying him, and that evening, when they went back home, he told his father that his brother and he were ready to do their duty: they had drawn lots, and he was the one to drive Father Caillaud's big oxen.

Father Barbeau took his twins on his knees—tall and heavy as they were—and said to them: "Children, you have reached years of discretion—I can see that, by your yielding to my wishes—and I am glad of it. Remember that when children obey their parents, they are obeying their Father in heaven, who will reward them for it some day or other. I do not care to know which one of you gave in first. But God knows, and He will bless him who made the proposal, as well as him who agreed to it."

So he led his twins to their mother to receive her approval, but Mother Barbeau had so much difficulty in restraining her tears that she could not speak to them, and only kissed them in silence.

Father Barbeau, who had plenty of sense, knew well enough which one of them was the most courageous and which the most affectionate. He did not want to give Sylvinet a chance to change his mind; for he saw that Landry had decided for himself and that the only thing which could make him waver in his determination would be the sight of his brother's distress.

So he woke Landry before daybreak, taking care not to rouse his brother, who was asleep at his side.

"Come, little one," said he, in a whisper; "we must start for La Priche before your mother sees you; for you know how she feels about your going away, and we must spare her a farewell. I am going with you to your new master's, and will carry your bundle."

"Won't you let me say goodbye to my brother?" asked Landry. "He will be angry with me if I go away without letting him know."

"If your brother should wake up and see you go, he will cry, and that will waken your mother, and your mother will feel all the worse at the sight of your grief. Come, Landry! You are a brave boy! You don't want to make your mother ill. Do your duty like a man, my son; go off without making any fuss. I will bring your brother to see you this evening, and, as tomorrow will be Sunday, you may come to see your mother as early as you please."

Landry obeyed like a hero and crossed the threshold without once looking back. Mother Barbeau was not so sound asleep that she had not heard all that her husband had said to Landry. The poor woman, acknowledging that her husband was right, did not stir, and only drew her curtain aside a little, so that she might see Landry go. She was so overcome with grief that she crawled out at the foot of the bed, intending to go and kiss him goodbye, but she stopped when she stood beside the twins' bed, where

Sylvinet was still asleep. The poor boy had cried so much for three days and almost three nights, that he was quite worn out, and even a little feverish, for he was tossing about on his pillow—sighing heavily and groaning, but without waking up.

Then Mother Barbeau, looking at the remaining twin, could not help acknowledging to herself that she would have felt worse to see this one go. It was true that he was the most affectionate of the two, perhaps because he was not quite so strong, or because God has established a natural law which decrees that when two persons have a very warm attachment to each other—be they friends or lovers—one always loves more intensely than the other. Father Barbeau had a slight partiality for Landry, because, in his eyes, a high spirit and an active and industrious disposition were of more value than winning manners and little endearing ways. But the mother had a special weakness for Sylvinet, who was more lovable and attractive.

So there she stood, looking at her poor boy, who was quite pale and exhausted, and saying to herself that it would have been a great pity to put him out to service so young; that Landry was stronger and better able to work, and, in addition to that, his fondness for his mother and his twin brother was not so great as to endanger his health.

"He is a child who has a great notion of duty," thought she; "but, all the same, he must be rather hard-hearted, or he would not have gone off like that, without a word of protest; never turning his head to look back, or shedding a tear. He would not have had the strength to go two steps without falling on his knees and praying Our Dear Lord to give him courage, and he would have come up to my bed, where I was pretending to be asleep if only to take one last look at me, and kiss the hem of my curtain. My Landry is every inch a boy! He cares for nothing but life and activity, and wants to run about and work, and have some change. But this one has the heart of a girl. He is so gentle and affectionate that one cannot help loving him like the apple of one's eye."

And so Mother Barbeau went on talking to herself, as she went back to bed, where she lay awake while Father Barbeau was taking Landry over fields and pastures towards La Priche. When they reached the brow of a hill, whence they could get a last view of the farm buildings of La Cosse, Landry stopped and looked back. His heart swelled; he seated himself on the fern and could not go a step farther. His father pretended not to notice him and walked on. In a moment or two, he called to him in a low voice: "See, Landry; it is daylight! We must hurry if we mean to get there before sunrise."

Landry rose, and, as if he had determined not to let his father see him cry, kept back the tears—as big as peas—which came into his eyes. He pretended that he was looking for his penknife, and reached La Priche without giving way to his grief, though it was hard enough to bear.

IV

Chapter 4

Father Caillaud, seeing that they had brought him the strongest and most industrious of the twins, received him very kindly. He knew well enough that it must have been very hard to decide upon this step, and as he was a good man and a kind neighbour, and also a great friend of Father Barbeau's, he did his best to encourage the youngster and cheer him up. He gave orders to bring him some soup at once, and a pitcher of wine to raise his spirits, for it was easy to see that he was very downhearted. Then he took him out to yoke up the oxen and showed him how it was done. Landry was not altogether a novice at this kind of work, for his father had a fine pair of oxen, which he had often yoked up, and which he drove remarkably well. As soon as the boy saw Father Caillaud's big oxen, which were the best cared for, the best fed, and the strongest breed of cattle in the country, he felt proud to think of having such fine beasts at the end of his goad. And then, too, he was glad of an opportunity to prove that he was neither timid nor awkward and that his duties were not new to him.

His father did not stint his praises, and when the time came to set out for the fields, all Father Caillaud's children, boys and girls, little and big, came and kissed the twin, and the youngest girl tied a bunch of flowers to his hat with a ribbon, because it was his first day at service and a kind of holiday for the whole family. Before leaving, his father gave him some advice in his new master's presence, telling him to be sure and try to please him in everything, and to take as good care of the cattle as if they belonged to him.

And so Landry went to work, after promising to do his best, and he kept up his courage and did good service all day, coming home with a fine appetite; for it was the first time that he had worked so hard, and there is no better remedy for grief than a little fatigue.

But time did not pass so rapidly at the Twinnery. As soon as Sylvinet woke, and saw that his brother was not at his side, he suspected what had happened, but could not believe that Landry would go off like that, without even saying goodbye to him; and his anger was almost equal to his grief. "What have I done to him," said he to his mother, "and how could I have displeased him? I have always done just what he told me to do, and when he urged me not to cry before you, darling mother, I kept back my tears, till I felt as if my head would burst. He promised me that he would not go away till he had said a few more encouraging words to me, and had taken breakfast with me at the other end of the hemp field—the place where we always used to go to play and have our little talks. I wanted to do up his bundle for him and to give him my knife, which is better than his. You did up his bundle yesterday evening, without saying anything about it to me, mother—did you know then that he was going away without saying goodbye to me?"

"I did as your father wished me to do," answered his mother.

And she said everything she could think of to comfort him. He would listen to nothing, and it was only when he saw that she was crying too, that he fell to kissing her, begged her pardon for adding to her troubles, and promised to stay with her to make amends. But as soon as she left him to attend to the poultry yard and the washing, he ran off in the direction of La Priche without even thinking where he was going, but obeying an instinct, just as a pigeon follows its mate, never heeding the road.

He would have gone all the way to La Priche, if he had not met his father coming back, who took him by the hand to lead him home, saying to him, "We will go over this evening, but we must not disturb your brother at his work; his master would not like that, and besides that, your mother is at home, and it is your place to comfort her."

V

Chapter 5

Sylvinet went back home and hung on his mother's petticoats as he had done when he was a little child, and never left her all day long, talking to her continually about Landry, not being able to stop thinking of him, and going into every nook and corner where they had been together. That evening he went over to La Priche with his father, who wanted to accompany him. Sylvinet was wild with impatience to embrace his brother, and he was so eager to get off that he could not eat any supper. He expected that Landry would come to meet him, and imagined every moment that he saw him running toward them. But Landry never stirred, much as he longed to do so. He was afraid that the young people at La Priche would ridicule the affection between the twins, which was looked upon as a sort of disease, so Sylvinet found him at the supper table, eating and drinking as if he had been a member of the Caillaud family all his life.

But Landry's heart leapt for joy when he saw him enter, and if he had not restrained himself, he would have upset table and bench in his eagerness to greet his brother. But he did not dare; for his master's family were watching him closely, much amused with the novelty of the relation, and with this natural phenomenon, as their schoolmaster called it. So Sylvinet rushed up to him, kissing him and crying over him, and cuddling up to him, as a bird nestles against its mate, to keep warm. Landry was provoked to have the others see him, though, as far as his own feelings were concerned, he could not help being delighted. He wished to appear more sensible than his brother and kept making signs to him to stop, much to Sylvinet's astonishment and distress. So, the twins went out together—Father Barbeau having seated himself to drink a couple of glasses of wine, and have a little chat with Father Caillaud. Landry was longing for an opportunity to kiss and hug his brother where nobody could see them, but the other boys were watching them from a distance, and even little Solange—Father Caillaud's youngest daughter, who was as mischievous and inquisitive as a linnet—trotted after them to the hazel copse, laughing shyly when they noticed her, but persisting, under the impression that she must be going to see something very extraordinary, though, to tell the truth, it did not seem to her so very remarkable that two brothers should love each other.

Sylvinet, though surprised at his brother's cool reception, never thought of reproaching him, so glad was he to be with him again.

Father Caillaud having told Landry that he might have a holiday the next day, he started off so early that he expected to surprise his brother in bed. But though Sylvinet was the heavier sleeper of the two, he waked just as Landry climbed the orchard fence, and ran out, barefooted, as if something had warned him that his twin was coming. It was a day of perfect delight to Landry; he was so glad to see his family and his home, for he knew that he could not go home every day, but must look upon it as a sort of reward of merit. The first half of the day, Sylvinet forgot all his sorrows. At breakfast time he looked forward to dining with his brother, but when dinner was over, he remembered that supper would be the last meal and began to be anxious and uneasy. He petted and coddled his brother to his heart's content, giving him all the titbits—the crusty bit of bread and the heart of the lettuce; and then he fell to worrying over Landry's clothes and shoes, as if he had a long distance to go, and was greatly to be pitied, never suspecting that he was himself more an object of compassion than Landry because he felt the separation most.

VI

⚜

Chapter 6

And so the week passed by, Sylvinet going to see Landry every day, and Landry stopping in for a moment or two whenever he came in the neighbourhood of the Twinnery; Landry becoming more and more reconciled to the separation, and Sylvinet, on the contrary, counting the days, the hours—like a soul in torment. Nobody in the world but Landry could make his brother listen to reason. Even his mother appealed to him to try and induce Sylvinet to be more reasonable, for the poor child's grief increased from day today. He would not play, he never worked unless told to do so; he still took his little sister out walking, but never spoke to her, and never did anything to amuse her, only taking care that she did not fall down and hurt herself. The moment nobody was looking, he went off alone and hid so cleverly that they could not find him. He scrambled into ditches, hedges, and ravines, where he and Landry used to play and chat; he sat

on the stumps where they had sat together and stuck his feet in
all the little streams where they had paddled about like a pair
of little ducklings. He was delighted when he found a few little
bits of wood which Landry had whittled with his garden knife or
some pebbles which he had used as quoits or flints. He gathered
them together and hid them in a hollow tree or under a brush
heap so that he might come and take them out every now and
then as if they were great treasures. He kept racking his brain to
recall anything which might serve to remind him of his past happiness. Such things would have meant nothing to anybody else,
but to him they meant everything. He gave no thought to the future, not daring to face the prospect of a long succession of days
such as he was now enduring. His thoughts were all in the past,
and he went about like one in a perpetual dream.

Sometimes he would fancy that he saw and heard his twin,
and then he talked to himself as if in answer to Landry. Or
he fell asleep wherever he might happen to be, dreaming about
him—and when he awoke, he wept to find himself alone, crying
with all his might, in hopes that fatigue would wear him out, and
so his pain would be eased.

One day when he had wandered as far as the coppice, he
found on the edge of the brook which ran through the wood
in the rainy season and which was now almost dried up, one
of those little mills which our children make out of twigs, and
which are so well constructed that they turn as the water runs
over them, and often last a long time, till they are destroyed
by other children, or swept away by the floods. The one which
Sylvinet found, quite safe and sound, had been there over two
months, and as it was a lonely nook, nobody had seen or injured

it. Sylvinet recognized it at once as his brother's work, and re-membered that when they had made it they had intended to come again and see it. But they had forgotten all about it, and since then they had made a good many mills in other places.

So Sylvinet was glad to find it again and carried it a little lower down, where there was more water, to see it turn, and re-call the pleasure which he and Landry had taken in setting it go-ing. And then he had left it there, intending to come back with Landry the next Sunday to show him how long their mill had lasted, because it was so well built. But he could not resist the temptation to come there alone the next day, and he found the edge of the brook all muddy and trampled by the hoofs of cat-tle, which had been turned out into the woods to pasture that morning and had come down to the brook to drink. He went a little farther, and saw that the cattle had trodden his mill un-derfoot, and crushed it into such tiny bits that he could find only a few of them. He felt very uneasy, and taking it into his head that Landry must have met with some mishap that day, he ran over to La Priche to convince himself that nothing had hap-pened to him. But, having noticed that Landry did not like to have him come to see him in the daytime, for fear that his mas-ter might think that he was wasting his time, and be displeased, he watched him from a distance and did not show himself. He would have been ashamed to confess what brought him there, and so went home without saying a word, and did not tell any-body till long afterwards.

As he grew pale, slept badly, and ate hardly anything, his mother was very much worried and did not know how to com-fort him. She tried taking him to market with her or sending him to the cattle fairs with his father and uncles, but nothing amused or interested him, and Father Barbeau, without saying anything to him about it, tried to persuade Father Caillaud to take both twins into his service. But Father Caillaud's reply was so sensible that he could not help agreeing with him.

"Just suppose that I should take them both for a time; it could not be for long, because while we need one helper, people like us cannot keep two. At the end of the year, you would have to hire one of them out to someone else. And don't you see that if your Sylvinet were in a place where they would make him work, he would have no time for moping, and would do as his brother does, who behaves himself like a little man? It must come to that sooner or later. Perhaps you may not be able to hire him out just where you would like, and if these children are to be further off from each other, and will not meet oftener than once a week or once a month, you had better begin at once, so that they may get used to not living in each other's pockets. Be sensible, old fellow, and don't pay so much attention to the whims of a child whom your wife and your other children have fondled and petted too much. The worst is over, and you may rest assured that he will soon get accustomed to the rest if you do not yield."

Father Barbeau gave in and acknowledged that the more Sylvinet saw of his twin, the more he would want to see. So, he determined that on next St. John's Day, he would try and hire him out, so that by seeing less and less of Landry, he would finally form a habit of living like other people, and not allow himself to be governed by an affection which was injuring his health.

But he could not talk about it yet to Mother Barbeau, for, at the first word, she would cry her eyes out. She said that it would be the death of Sylvinet, and so Father Barbeau was in a great quandary.

Landry, by the advice of his father, his mother, and also his master, tried to reason with his poor twin. Sylvinet had nothing to say for himself; he promised to do just what they wanted him to do, but could not control his feelings. There was another trouble of which he said nothing because he was at a loss how to express himself. In the very bottom of his heart, he was jealous of Landry. Nothing pleased him more than to see that everybody liked Landry and that his new master and mistress treated him as kindly as if he were their own child. But if, on the one hand, he was delighted at this, on the other, it annoyed him when Landry seemed too fond of these new friends. He could not bear to see him run off at a word from Father Caillaud, no matter how gentle the summons or how much against his will it might be, leaving his father, mother, or brother, more afraid of being delinquent in duty than in affection, and more prompt in obedience than Sylvinet could conceive of being when it was a question of remaining a few moments longer with the objects of such devoted love.

Then the poor child was seized with a fear that had not troubled him till now. It seemed to him that the love was all on one side. That it was ill-requited; that this must always have been the case, though he had not been conscious of it, or, rather, that for some time back his brother's love for him had cooled because he had met people who were more congenial to him, and whom he found more agreeable.

VII

Chapter 7

Landry did not suspect that his brother was jealous, for he had never in his life known what it is to be jealous of anybody or anything. When Sylvinet came to see him at La Priche, Landry entertained him by taking him to see the big oxen, the fine cows, the large flocks of sheep, and the abundant crops of Father Caillaud's farm. Landry attached great value to all these things, not that he was envious, but because he had a real taste for farming and cattle raising, and for everything which is attractive in country life. He liked to see the colt, which he led to pasture, look clean and fat and sleek, and he could not bear to see the smallest piece of work neglected, nor any gift of Our Dear Lord disregarded or despised if it was capable of living and flourishing. Sylvinet cared nothing for all these things, and could not understand how they could have any interest for his brother. He took offence at everything, and said to Landry, "You seem to be very much taken with those big oxen. You don't care anymore for our little bullocks who are so high-spirited and yet so gentle with us two, that they would let you yoke them up sooner than they would our father. You haven't even asked after our cow which gives such good milk, and who looks at me so sadly, poor beast, when I go to feed her, as if she understood that I am all alone, and wanted to ask me what has become of the other twin."

"She is a good cow, that's true," said Landry, "but just look at this one! You shall see them milk her, and you never in your life saw so much milk at once."

"That may be," answered Sylvinet, "but I bet it is not such good cream and milk as Brunette's, for the grazing at the Twinnery is better than the grazing about here."

"The deuce, it is!" said Landry. "Don't you suppose that my father would be glad to exchange if he could get Father Caillaud's fine hayfields instead of his rush field down by the water ?"

"Pooh!" retorted Sylvinet, shrugging his shoulders. "There are finer trees in the rush field than any of yours, and as for the hay, if there isn't much of it, it is fine, and when it is harvested it leaves a perfume like balm all along the road."

And so they disputed about nothing, for Landry knew well enough that nobody's property is so fine as one's own, and Sylvinet, in depreciating the La Priche land, was not thinking of his own or anybody else's. But under all these idle words, there was, on the one hand, the boy who was willing to work and live anywhere or anyhow, and, on the other hand, the boy who could not understand how his brother could enjoy a moment's ease and comfort away from him.

If Landry took him into his master's garden and interrupted

their conversation to cut off a dead branch from a grafted tree, or to pull up a weed which had grown up among the vegetables, Sylvinet got angry to see that he was always thinking of the interests of others, instead of being, like himself, at his brother's beck and call. He kept this to himself because he was ashamed of being so touchy, but when he left, he often said to Landry: "Well, you've had enough of me today—perhaps too much; maybe it bores you to have me come here."

Landry did not understand these reproaches, but they hurt his feelings, and in return, he reproached his brother, who either could not or would not explain himself. If the poor child was jealous of the slightest thing which interested Landry, he was still more jealous of the people to whom Landry seemed to be attached. He could not bear to see Landry on friendly terms with the other boys at La Priche, and when he saw him taking care of little Solange—petting or playing with her—he accused him of forgetting his little sister Nanette, who was, in his opinion, a hundred times prettier, cleaner and sweeter than that ugly little girl.

But—as one is never just when one is eaten up by jealousy—when Landry came over to the Twinnery, it seemed to him that he took too much notice of his little sister. Sylvinet accused him of devoting himself altogether to her, and of manifesting nothing but indifference toward himself.

In fact, his affection became by degrees so exacting, and he was so dull and melancholy, that Landry began to find it disagreeable and did not care to see too much of him. He was rather tired of his perpetual reproaches for having accepted his lot as he had done, and it certainly seemed as if Sylvinet would be less miserable if he could make his brother as miserable as himself. Landry saw and tried to make him see, that excessive affection is sometimes injurious. Sylvinet would not believe it and even thought that his brother was very cruel to speak to him so. And so, he would have an occasional fit of the sulks, and sometimes would not come to La Priche for weeks at a time, though he was longing to go there, and was acting entirely from a false sense of pride.

And so it came to pass that, one word leading to another, and quarrel begetting quarrel, Sylvinet always taking in bad part all Landry's kind and sensible efforts to bring him to a better frame of mind, poor Sylvinet became so perverse that he took it into his head to hate his brother whom he had so dearly loved, and one Sunday he left the house, so as not to spend the day with Landry, who had not once missed coming.

This piece of childish naughtiness was very distressing to Landry. He was fond of gayety and he loved fun and frolic, for he grew stronger and more independent day by day. He led in every game, for he had a keener eye and a more agile body than his comrades. So it was something of a sacrifice which he made for his brother's sake, when he left the merry boys at La Priche, to spend every Sunday at the Twinnery with Sylvinet, who would not hear of going out to play on the public square of La Cosse, or taking a walk in the neighbourhood. Sylvinet, who was much more childish in mind and body than his brother, and whose one idea was to love and be loved in return, wanted him to go off all alone to what he called *their* places, the nooks and corners where they used to play at those games which were no longer suited to their age, such as making little wheelbarrows of osier, or little mills, or snares to catch little birds; or, perhaps, building houses out of pebbles, or laying out fields the size of a handkerchief, which children make believe to cultivate in all sorts of ways, imitating on a small scale what they see done by the ploughmen, sowers, harrowers, weeders, and reapers, and thus teaching each other in an hour's time all the different modes of cultivation, and the rotation of crops which the earth bears in the course of a year.

These amusements were no longer to Landry's taste, now that he practised or helped to practise them on a large scale, and he liked far better to drive a large cart with six oxen than to fasten a little wagon made of twigs to his dog's tail. He would much rather have gone and played skittles with the stout boys in the neighbourhood, now that he was skilful enough to lift the big ball and make it hit the goal at thirty paces. When he got Sylvinet to go with him, he sat in a corner and would neither play nor say a word, ready to take offence and sulk, if it seemed to him that Landry showed too great pleasure and interest in the game.

Landry had also learned to dance at La Priche, and although he had never cared for this amusement till now because Sylvinet did not like it, he already danced as well as those who had been used to dancing ever since they could walk. At La Priche they considered him a good jig or bourrée dancer, and though, as yet, he did not take any pleasure in kissing the girls, as was customary in every figure, he was quite willing to do it because it made him appear more manly, and he even wished that the girls would pretend to make a fuss about it as they did with the men. But they did not as yet, and some of the biggest ones even threw their arms about his neck and laughed, much to his annoyance.

Sylvinet had once seen him dance, and that had been the cause of one of his worst fits of ill-humour. He was so angry when he saw him kiss one of Father Caillaud's daughters, that he shed tears of jealousy, and thought the whole proceeding very unkind and improper.

And so, each time that Landry sacrificed his own enjoyment to his brother's exacting affection for him, he spent a rather dull Sunday; yet he never failed to come, knowing that it would gratify Sylvinet, and willing to be bored a little for the sake of giving his brother some pleasure.

So when he found that his brother, who had picked a quarrel with him during the week, had left the house so as not to make up with him, it was his turn to feel hurt, and for the first time since he had left home, he went off and hid himself to have a good cry; for he was ashamed to let his parents see how much he felt Sylvinet's conduct and did not wish to add to their troubles.

If anybody had cause for jealousy, it was Landry, far more than Sylvinet. Sylvinet was his mother's favourite, and even Father Barbeau, though in his heart he preferred Landry, was more indulgent to Sylvinet. The poor child, being more delicate and not so bright, was also more spoiled, and they did not like to cross him. His lot was the easier, for he lived at home and his twin had sacrificed himself to save him from leaving his parents and earning his living by hard work.

This was the first time that Landry had taken this view of the matter, and had come to the conclusion that his brother was treating him with great injustice. Hitherto his kind heart had prevented him from blaming Sylvinet and, rather than accuse him, he had thought that it must be his own fault—that he was too overflowing with health and spirits, too fond of work and of pleasure, and not so dependent on delicate attentions as his brother. But this time he could not discover that he had been guilty of any offence against their mutual affection; for by coming today, he had missed a delightful crabbing party which the La Priche boys had been planning all the week, and which they told him he would be sure to enjoy if he would only go with them. So, he had resisted a great temptation, and at his age, that is saying a good deal. When he had been crying a long time, he stopped to listen to someone else, who was also crying not far off, and talking to herself as our peasant women often do when in trouble. Landry knew at once that it was his mother, and hastened to join her.

"Oh, for the love of heaven, why does this child make me suffer so? He will surely be the death of me!" said she, sobbing.

"Do I make you suffer?" exclaimed Landry, throwing his arms around her neck. "If it is my fault, punish me, but don't cry! I don't know what I can have done to displease you, but I beg your pardon, all the same."

Then his mother saw that Landry was not so hard-hearted as she had so often imagined. She kissed him tenderly, and hardly knowing what she said, she was so agitated, she told him that it was not he but Sylvinet who had grieved her; that although she had sometimes done him an injustice, she now wished to make amends for it; but that Sylvinet seemed to have lost his senses, and she was very unhappy about him because he had gone off before daylight, without taking anything to eat. It was now near sunset, and he had not yet returned. He had been seen about noonday, down by the river, and at last Mother Barbeau began to fear that he had drowned himself.

VIII

Chapter 8

Landry's imagination caught at this notion of his mother's, that Sylvinet might have made way with himself, as quickly as a spider's web catches a fly, and he at once set out in search of his brother. He felt very unhappy as he ran along, and said to himself: "Perhaps my mother was right when she accused me of being hard-hearted. But surely Sylvinet must be hard-hearted too, or he would not cause my mother and me so much anxiety."

He ran about in all directions without seeing anything of him—asking after him from everyone he met, calling him without getting any answer; but all was in vain. At last, he came to the rush field, and went in, knowing that one of Sylvinet's haunts was there. It was a deep hollow where the river had washed away two or three alder trees, which still lay with their roots uppermost. Father Barbeau would not have them removed. He let them stay there because they had fallen in such a way that the earth still adhered to their roots, which was very lucky; for every winter the water did a great deal of damage in his rush field, and he lost a good bit of land each year.

So, Landry ran over to the "Hollow" as he and his brother called that part of their rush field. He did not take time to go to the corner where they had built themselves a little stairway of sods, supported by stones, and big roots which protruded from the earth and sent out young shoots. He jumped down at the first place he came to, so as to get to the bottom of the Hollow as soon as possible; for the grass and bushes along the river bank were so much taller than he, that even if his brother had been there, he could not have found him by looking down from above.

So, he entered the Hollow, feeling very anxious; for he could not help thinking of what his mother had said about the possibility of Sylvinet's having drowned himself. He went in and out among the bushes, beating the grass, calling Sylvinet, and whistling to the dog, which had probably followed him; for he had been gone all day, as well as his young master.

But in spite of all his efforts, there was none but himself to be found in the Hollow. As he was a very observing boy and did everything very thoroughly, he examined the banks to see if he could find any footprints or any place where the earth seemed to be disturbed. It was an anxious and troublesome search; for Landry had not been there for over a month, and though he knew each nook and corner of the ground as well as he did his own hand, it was impossible that there should not have been some slight change. The entire right bank was covered with turf, and even at the bottom of the Hollow the rushes and horsetails had grown up so rank and luxuriant, that there was not a bare spot big enough to hold a footprint.

However, after a long search, Landry found the impress of a dog's paw in a remote corner. There was also a spot where the grass had been trampled down, as if Finot, or some other dog of his size, had lain there curled up. This attracted his notice, and he made a still more minute examination of the river bank. He found what seemed to him a fresh break as if made by the foot of a person jumping or sliding down the slope, though it was quite possible that it was the work of one of those big water rats, which scratch and dig and gnaw in such places. He was so alarmed that his legs refused to carry him, and he fell on his knees as if to ask for help from heaven.

He remained in this position for a short time, having neither strength nor courage to go and tell anybody what had caused his alarm, and gazing at the river with tearful eyes, as if asking what had become of his brother. And all the while the river flowed tranquilly on, swaying the branches of the trees which hung over its banks, dipping their twigs in its waters, and pursuing its course through the fields, murmuring low to itself, with a sound like mocking laughter.

Poor Landry was so possessed with the idea that some terrible misfortune had occurred, that he lost his head completely, and magnified a trifle which was, no doubt, quite easy to explain, till it drove him to absolute desperation. "This wicked river which will not answer me," thought he, "and which would let me go on weeping a whole year, without giving me back my brother, is deepest just at that place and is so filled with stumps since the time of the inundation, that it would be impossible to get out again if one should fall in. Great God! Can it be possible that my twin is in there, under the water, lying scarcely two feet away from me and I could never find him among the reeds and branches even if I should go down there!"

So, he began to weep for his brother, and to reproach him, for never in his life had he been so unhappy.

At last, it occurred to him to consult a widow, named Mother Fadet, who lived at the other end of the rush field, near the road which led down to the ford. This woman, whose only property consisted of her little garden and house, never lacked for bread; for she was very learned in all that relates to human ills and mishaps, and people came from far and near to consult her. She was a magic healer; that is to say, she cured wounds, bruises, and all sorts of fractures, by means known only to herself. Indeed, she took rather too much upon herself, for she claimed to be able to cure diseases which never existed; such as displacement of the stomach, or rupture of the abdominal wall, and I must say I have never put much faith in the possibility of such ailments, any more than I could believe that she had the power to cause a good cow's milk to pass into the body of a poor one, however old or ill-fed she might be.

But there is no doubt she earned her money honestly by her excellent remedies for chills, her healing plasters for cuts and burns, and the potions which she concocted to allay fever, and that she had saved many a patient whom the doctors would have killed, had they been allowed to prescribe for them. At least, so she said, and those whom she had benefited thought best to believe her, instead of expressing any doubts. As country folks always suspect anyone who has any special skill of being in league with the devil, many people believed that Mother Fadet knew much more than she was willing to tell, and it was said that she could find lost things and even persons. In fact, because she was clever enough to be able to assist people in natural and possible ways, they took it for granted that she could do the same in things beyond human ken.

As children listen eagerly to all sorts of stories, Landry had heard from the La Priche folks, who are known to be more simple-minded and credulous than they are at La Cosse, that Mother Fadet could find the body of a person who had been drowned, by means of a certain seed which she threw into the water, pronouncing a spell as she did so. The seed floated on the surface of the water, and the poor body was certain to be found where it stopped. There are many persons who believe that blessed bread has the same wonderful properties, and there are few mills where they do not keep a supply on hand for such emergencies. But Landry had none; Mother Fadet lived close by the rush field, and there is no time for reflection when one is in such distress.

So off he ran to Mother Fadet's dwelling, and told her the trouble he was in, and begged her to come to the Hollow with him, and use her magic to find his brother, alive or dead.

But Mother Fadet, who did not care to risk her reputation, and was not at all disposed to exercise her talents for nothing, laughed at him, and ordered him away harshly enough; for she had taken great offence when the family at the Twinnery had employed La Sagette as nurse in preference to herself, as had happened more than once in the past.

Landry, who had his own share of pride, would probably, at

any other time, have protested or given her a sharp answer, but he was so agitated that he had not a word to say and started to go back to the Hollow, determined to jump into the water, though he could neither dive nor swim. But as he trudged along with drooping head, and eyes fixed on the ground, he felt a tap on his shoulder, and turning round saw Mother Fadet's granddaughter, whom the country people called little Fadette, as much because she was herself a bit of a witch as because it was her family name. As you all know, the *fadet* or the *farfadet*, which in other places is called the will-o'-the-wisp, is a very pretty little sprite though rather mischievous. Fairies are also called *fades* in our part of the country, though nobody believes in them nowadays. But whether they meant a little fairy or a female spirit, nobody could look at her without thinking of a will-o'-the-wisp—she was so little, so thin, so dishevelled and so bold. She was a very talkative and saucy child, lively as a butterfly, inquisitive as a robin redbreast, and brown as a cricket.

And when I compare little Fadette to a cricket, I mean to say that she was not pretty; for this poor little field chirper is still uglier than his brother of the chimney-corner. If, however, you can remember how you used to play with them when you were a child, teasing them and making them chirp angrily in your sabot, you must know that they have queer, intelligent little faces, which make you feel more like laughing at them than getting angry. So the children of La Cosse, who were as clever as other children and as quick to notice resemblances and make comparisons, called little Fadette the "Cricket," when they wanted to make her mad, and sometimes by way of a pet name; for though they stood a little in awe of her on account of her impish ways, they did not dislike her, for she told them all sorts of stories and was always teaching them new games which she had the wit to invent.

But all these names and nicknames have made me forget to mention the one which was bestowed upon her in baptism, and which you would perhaps like to know later on. Her name was Françoise, and so her grandmother, who did not like nicknames, called her Fanchon.

As there was a coolness of long-standing between the Twinnery folks and Mother Fadet, the twins never talked much to little Fadette; indeed, they rather avoided her, and never cared to play with her or her little brother, the "Grasshopper," who was more dried up and impish-looking than his sister, and was always hanging on to her skirts, flying into a rage when she ran off without waiting for him, trying to throw stones at her when she teased him, getting more furious than would seem possible for one of his size and provoking her in spite of herself, for she was a merry little thing and ready to laugh at anything. But there was such an impression prevailing about Mother Fadet that some people, especially the Barbeaus, fancied that the Cricket and the Grasshopper would bring them some ill luck if they made friends with them. This did not prevent the two children from speaking to them, for they were not bashful, and little Fadette never failed to call out all sorts of nicknames and nonsense after the twins of the Twinnery, as far off as she could see them.

IX

Chapter 9

So poor Landry turned around, rather irritated by the tap on his shoulder, and saw little Fadette, and not far behind her, Jeanet, the Grasshopper, hobbling along after her, for he had been born with a misshapen body and crooked legs.

At first, Landry refused to take any notice of them, but kept right on, for he was in no mood for fun-making; but Fadette said to him, tapping him on the other shoulder: "Wolf! Wolf! you naughty twin; you half a boy, who has lost his other half!" Thereupon Landry, who was no more in the mood to be insulted than to stand teasing, turned and aimed a blow of his fist at little Fadette, which would have hurt her, had she not dodged aside; for the twin was going on fifteen, and knew the use of his arms, and she, though nearly fourteen, was so slender and delicate that she did not look more than twelve, and seemed as if she would break in two if you touched her.

But she was too nimble and too much on her guard to stand still and take his blows, and what she lacked in strength she made up in agility and cunning. She dodged so cleverly around a big tree, that Landry came near running his nose and his fist against it. "You good-for-nothing Cricket!" cried Landry, in a rage. "You must be perfectly heartless to try and torment anyone who is in such trouble as I am! You've been teasing me this long while back, by calling me a half-boy, and I have a great mind to break you and your ugly Grasshopper into quarters, to see if both of you together would make a quarter of anything decent."

"Indeed, my fine twin of the Twinnery! Lord of the rush field on the river bank!" answered little Fadette, sneering at him again. "You are a great fool to quarrel with me just when I was about to give you some news of your twin and tell you where to find him."

"That is a different thing," said Landry, quieting down at once. "Do tell me, Fadette, if you know; I shall be so thankful."

"Fadette doesn't care to please you any more than the Cricket did a little while ago," answered the little girl. "You have been abusing me, and you would have struck me if you had not been so awkward and clumsy. Go and find your fool of a brother yourself, if you know so much about it."

"I am a fool to listen to you, you wicked girl," said Landry, turning his back on her, and walking on. "You don't know where my brother is any more than I do, and you are no wiser than your grandmother, who is an old liar and as worthless as she can be."

But little Fadette, dragging her little Grasshopper along by one claw—for he had managed to catch up to her and was hanging on to her ragged, ash-covered petticoats—followed on behind Landry, jeering at him and telling him that he would never find his brother without her help. So Landry, not being able to get rid of her and fancying that she or her grandmother—by some piece of witchcraft or by connivance with the will-o'-the-wisp of the river—might prevent his finding Sylvinet, determined to take a short cut across the rush field and go home.

Little Fadette followed him to the turnstile which led into the meadow, and when he had crossed it, she perched herself on the top rail like a magpie and called after him: "Goodbye, you pretty, hard-hearted twin who leaves his brother behind him. You may wait supper as long as you like, you won't see him today or tomorrow either! He can't stir from where he is, any more than a stone, and there is a storm coming up! There will be more trees in the river tonight, and the river will carry Sylvinet away, so far, so far that you will never find him again!"

These spiteful words, to which Landry could not help listening, made a cold sweat break out all over his body. He did not absolutely believe them, but the Fadet family had so well established a reputation for dealings with the devil, that one could not be certain that there was nothing in it.

"See here, Fanchon!" said Landry, standing still, "tell me, yes or no, will you leave me alone, or say whether you really know anything about my brother!"

"And what will you give me if I help you find your brother before it begins to rain?" asked Fadette, standing on the top rail and waving her arms as if about to fly.

Landry did not know what to promise her, but he began to think that she was trying to get some money out of him. But the wind whistling through the trees, and the distant rumble of thunder worked him up into a perfect panic. It was not that he was afraid of an ordinary storm, but this one had come up so suddenly and in a way which seemed to him supernatural. It may be that in his agitation Landry had not noticed it gathering behind the trees along the river bank, particularly as, having spent two hours in the Hollow down by the Val, he had not been able to see the sky till he had reached high ground. But, however that may be, he had not noticed that there was a storm brewing till the moment when little Fadette announced it, when, lo and behold, out flew her skirt, her ugly black bait escaped from under her cap, which was always untied and tilted over one ear, and stood out like a mane.

The Grasshopper's cap was carried away by a gust, and Landry had all that he could do to keep his hat from following it.

In less than two minutes the sky had grown very black, and Fadette, standing on the rail, looked twice as tall as usual; in short, we may as well own that Landry was frightened. "Fanchon," said he, "I will give in if you will give me back my brother. Maybe you've seen him and know where he is. Come, be a good girl! I can't see what pleasure you can take in seeing me suffer. Show me that you have a kind heart, and I will believe that you are better than one would suppose from your looks and words."

"And why should I be a good girl to please you?" answered she, "when you treat me as if I were a bad girl, though I have never done anything to you? Why should I be good to twins who are as proud as peacocks, and who have never shown me the least little bit of kindness?"

"Come, Fadette," said Landry, "you want me to promise you

something. Tell me quick what you want, and I will give it to you. Would you like to have my new knife?"

"Let me see it," cried Fadette, leaping down beside him like a frog.

When she had seen the knife, which was a pretty good one, for which Landry's godfather had paid ten sous at the last fair, she was tempted for a moment. But she soon decided it was not enough, and asked him if he would give her instead his little white hen which was no bigger than a pigeon and had feathers down to the very tips of its toes.

"I can't promise you my white hen, because she belongs to my mother," answered Landry, " but I promise that I will ask her to give it to you, and I am sure that she won't refuse, for she will be so glad to get Sylvinet back again that she will not grudge you anything."

"Indeed!" said little Fadette, "and what if I should take it into my head to ask for your black-nosed kid; would Mother Barbeau give me that too?"

"Good heavens! How long it takes you to make up your mind, Fanchon! Listen! There are no two words about it? If my brother is in danger, and you take me to him at once, I am very sure there is not a hen or a chicken, a goat or a kid, about the place, which my father and mother would not gladly give you as a reward."

"Well! We'll see about it, Landry," said little Fadette, holding out her scrawny little hand to the boy, so that they might shake hands on their bargain, which he did, but not without fear and trembling; for at that moment her eyes glowed so that she looked a very incarnation of the will-o'-the-wisp. "I will not tell you what I want of you! Perhaps I have not yet made up my mind; but don't forget what you have promised me, and if you do not keep your promise to me, I shall tell everybody that there is no trusting the word of Landry, the twin. So now goodbye, and don't forget that I shall not ask you for anything till the day when I take it into my head to hunt you up and demand something which you must place at my disposal at once, and with good grace."

"All right, Fadette! I promise you; it is a bargain," said Landry, shaking hands with her. "Well," said she, looking quite pleased and proud, "go back to the riverbank, and keep on till you hear a bleating, and where you see a black lamb, you will see your brother too. If it doesn't turn out as I tell you, I let you off your promise."

And then the Cricket, tucking the Grasshopper under her arm, and never heeding his struggles, for he wriggled like an eel, ran off into the bushes, and Landry saw or heard no more of them than if it had all been a dream. He wasted no time wondering whether little Fadette had been making fun of him. He hurried to the other end of the rush field, without drawing breath; he ran along its border till he reached the Hollow, and then he was about to go on without stopping, as he had already examined the spot so closely that he was sure Sylvinet was not there, but just at that moment he heard the bleating of a lamb.

"Oh, my God! "thought he, "that girl told the truth. I hear the lamb, my brother must be there, but I don't know whether he is dead or alive!"

He jumped down into the Hollow and pushed his way through the bushes. His brother was not there but following the stream for ten paces or so, still hearing the lamb bleat, Landry saw his brother sitting on the opposite bank, holding a little lamb in his blouse, which was indeed quite black, from the tip of its nose to the end of its tail.

As Sylvinet was very much alive indeed and bore no traces of any injury about his clothes or his person, Landry was so overjoyed that he fell to thanking God in his heart, and never thought of asking pardon for having resorted to the assistance of the devil, that he might attain this happiness. But as he was about to call out to Sylvinet, who had not yet seen him, and did not appear to have heard him, on account of the rippling of the water over the stones, he paused to take a look at him; for he was amazed to find him just as little Fadette had predicted, sitting as still as a stone among the trees, through which the wind was howling like a tempest.

Everyone knows that it is dangerous to remain close to our river when the wind is blowing hard. All its banks are undermined, and there is not a storm which does not uproot some of the many alder trees, which always have short roots, unless they are very large and old, and which are likely to fall on you without any warning. But Sylvinet, though he had as good sense as the next one, did not seem to be aware of his danger. He appeared to think himself as safe as if he had taken shelter in a good barn. Tired out with his all-day tramp, and his aimless wanderings, though, as it happened, he had not drowned himself in the river, it was easy enough to see that he was so overwhelmed with grief and so heavy-hearted that he lay there like a log, his eyes fixed on the stream, his face as pale as a waterlily, his mouth half-open like a little fish gaping at the sun, his hair blown about by the wind, and not even taking any notice of the lamb, which he had found roaming about in the meadow, and had carried with him out of pity. He had put it in his blouse, intending to return it to its owner, but had forgotten to ask along the road to whom the lamb belonged. He let it lie on his lap and did not listen to its bleating, though the poor little thing kept up a most mournful noise, and looked about with its big, bright eyes, wondering that none of its kindred were there to hear its cries. This shady spot, all overgrown with grass, beside a large stream of water, which, no doubt, seemed very alarming to the poor little beast, looked very unfamiliar, and not at all like its native meadow, where were its mother and its fold.

X

Chapter 10

If Landry had not been separated from Sylvinet by the river, which is nowhere more than four or five yards wide, but which at some points is as deep as it is broad, he would certainly have rushed into his brother's arms, without a moment's hesitation. But as Sylvinet had not even seen him, he had time to think how he might rouse him from his meditations, and persuade him to go home; for if the poor, sulky boy should not be willing to go, he could easily run away, and it would take Landry some time to find a ford or a footbridge so as to follow him. So Landry, after thinking it over a little while, tried to imagine what his father would have done in such a case; for he knew him to be a sensible man, with prudence enough for four. Luckily, he came to the conclusion that Father Barbeau would take it very quietly, pretending that there was nothing out of the way, so as not to let Sylvinet know how much anxiety he had caused, that he might neither repent it too bitterly nor be disposed to try it again the next time anything happened to offend him.

So, he began to whistle as if trying to make the blackbirds sing, just as the shepherd boys do when they go through the bushes at nightfall. This made Sylvinet raise his head, and when he saw his brother, he was ashamed of himself, and got up at once, thinking that Landry had not seen him. Then Landry pretended, that he had just caught sight of him, and called to him in his ordinary tone of voice, for the river did not make enough noise to prevent their talking to each other: "Hello, Sylvinet! Is that you? I waited for you all the morning, and finding that you had gone out for such a long time, I walked over here while they were getting supper, and expected to find you at home when I went back. But now that you are here, we'll go back together. We can go down the river, one on either side, and we'll meet at the Roulettes ford."

"Come along," said Sylvinet, picking up his lamb, which did not know him well enough to follow of its own accord, and they walked down the river, not daring to look at each other; for neither wished the other to see how much he had suffered on account of the quarrel nor how glad he was to see his brother once more. Every now and then Landry said a word or two as they walked along so that he might not appear to notice his brother's sullen mood. First, he asked him where he had found the little black lamb, and Sylvinet rather evaded the question, for he did not even know the names of the places through which he had passed. So then, Landry, seeing his embarrassment, said to him, "You may tell me all about it by and by, for the wind is high, and it is dangerous to stay among the trees by the river. But luckily it is beginning to rain, and the wind will soon fall."

And he said to himself, "The Cricket was right when she said that I should find him before the rain began. That girl certainly does know more than the rest of us."

He did not take into consideration that he had wasted fully a quarter of an hour explaining his errand to Mother Fadet—she refusing to listen to his entreaties—and that little Fadette, whom he had not seen till he was coming out of the house, might very readily have caught sight of Sylvinet during that explanation. At length, it occurred to him to wonder how she had known so well what he was worrying about when she spoke to him, for she had not been present during his conversation with the old woman. He forgot that, on his way from the rush field, he had inquired of several persons whether they had seen his brother, and that very likely someone had mentioned it before little Fadette, or that perhaps the little girl might have overheard the conclusion of his conversation with her grandmother—hiding, as she was in the habit of doing so that she might gratify her curiosity. Now Sylvinet, on the other hand, was wondering how he could explain his bad behaviour to his mother and brother; for Landry's ruse had taken him by surprise, and he could not think of anything to say—he who had never told a lie in his life, and who had never kept anything from his brother.

So, he felt very uneasy as he crossed the ford, for he had not yet thought of any excuse to make. As soon as he reached the opposite bank, Landry embraced him, and, in spite of himself, he could not help showing more affection than usual. But he refrained from asking any questions, for he saw plainly enough that Sylvinet had nothing to say for himself, and on the way home he talked about every imaginable thing but the subject uppermost in the minds of both. As he passed Mother Fadet's house, he looked about for little Fadette, for he felt as if he should like to go and thank her. But the door was shut, and there was no sound to be heard, except the Grasshopper howling because his grandmother had thrashed him, which she did every evening, whether he had done anything to deserve it or not.

Sylvinet was worried when he heard the young scamp crying, and said to his brother: "You always hear screaming and the sound of blows from that abominable house. I know the Grasshopper is as naughty and provoking as he can be, and as for the Cricket, I wouldn't give two cents for her. But those poor children have no father or mother, and are dependent on that old witch, who is always in a bad humour, and never overlooks anything they do."

"That isn't the way at our house," answered Landry. "Our father and mother have never given us a whipping in our lives, and even when they scolded us for some childish piece of mischief, they did it so quietly and gently that the neighbours could not hear them. There are some people who don't know when they are well off, and yet little Fadette, who is the most unfortunate and ill-used child on earth, is always laughing, and never utters a complaint."

Sylvinet took the hint and was sorry for what he had done. He had repented many a time since morning, and more than twenty times had he been on the point of going home, but shame had held him back. Now his breast heaved, and he wept silently.

But his brother took him by the hand and said to him, "It is raining hard, Sylvinet, let us run a race to the house!"

So, they began to run, Landry trying to make Sylvinet laugh, and Sylvinet forcing a smile to please him.

Yet when they reached the house, Sylvinet had a great mind to go and hide in the barn; for he was afraid that his father would reprove him. But Father Barbeau, who did not take things so seriously as his wife did, only laughed at him; and Mother Barbeau, who had had a long talk with her husband, tried not to let Sylvinet see how anxious she had been about him. But while she was drying her twins in front of the fire, and giving them their supper, Sylvinet noticed that every now and then she gave him a look full of distress and anxiety.

Had he been alone with her, he would have begged her pardon and consoled her with his caresses, but his father disapproved of such blandishments, and Sylvinet did not get an opportunity to say a word to her, for he was so overcome with fatigue, that he had to go to bed immediately after supper. He had eaten nothing all day, and as soon as he had swallowed his supper—of which he stood greatly in need—he felt as if he were tipsy, and his twin had to undress him and put him to bed, but sat down on the edge of the bed beside him, holding his hand.

When he saw that Sylvinet was sound asleep, Landry said goodnight to his parents, and never noticed that his mother kissed him more tenderly than usual. He always believed that she could not love him as well as she did his brother, and he was not in the least jealous; for he thought that he was not so lovable as Sylvinet and that he got his full share of his mother's affection. He resigned himself to this, as much to show respect to his mother, as out of love for his brother, who stood more in need of petting and coddling than he did. The next morning Sylvinet ran to Mother Barbeau's bed before she was up, and opened his heart to her, confessing his sorrow and shame. He told her how unhappy he had been for some time past, not so much on account of his separation from Landry, as because he fancied that Landry no longer loved him. And when his mother asked him why he was so unjust to Landry, he could give no reason; for it seemed to be a kind of disease, which he found it impossible to resist. His mother understood him better than she allowed him to suspect; for a woman's heart is prone to such torments, and she had herself often suffered when she saw how self-reliant and independent Landry was. But now she realized how wrong it is to allow oneself to be jealous even in those relations of life which have the express sanction of God, and she took good care not to encourage this feeling in Sylvinet. She pointed out to him how much trouble he had caused his brother, and how kind Landry had been not to complain of him, or seem out of patience with him. Sylvinet agreed with her and owned that his brother was a better Christian than himself. He promised and vowed that he would cure himself of this fault, and he was thoroughly in earnest.

But do what he would—though he tried to seem happy and contented, though his mother had dried his tears and soothed his woes, and though he did his utmost to treat his brother naturally and justly—there was still a little leaven of bitterness fermenting in his heart.

He could not help saying to himself, "My brother is a better Christian than I am, and he is more upright and honourable. My mother says so, and it is true, but if he were as fond of me as I am of him, he could never have given in as he has done."

And then he remembered how cool and indifferent Landry had seemed when he found him by the river. How he had heard him whistling to the blackbirds while he was looking for him, at the very moment when he, Sylvinet, was thinking of throwing himself into the river. For though he had no idea of such a thing when he left home, it had occurred to him more than once toward evening; for he thought that his brother would never forgive him because he had gone off in a fit of the sulks, and had avoided him as he had never done before.

"If he had treated me so," thought he, "I should never have forgotten it. I am very glad that he has forgiven me, but I did not expect that he would forgive me so readily."

Then the poor child sighed in his efforts to struggle against his unhappy weakness, and his struggles did not cease with his sighs.

However, as God always rewards and assists those who try to please Him, Sylvinet really was more sensible for the remainder of the year. He did not sulk or quarrel with his brother; in fact, his love was more moderate, and his health, which had been impaired by all this distress of mind, was re-established, and he began to gain strength. His father gave him more work to do, noticing that the less time he had for thinking, the better he felt. But it is always easier to work for one's parents than to work elsewhere for hire, and Landry, who did not spare himself, increased so in strength and size that year, that he far outstripped his brother. The slight points of difference between them became more marked and passed from their moral natures to their physical. By the time they had completed their fifteenth year, Landry was a fine-looking young man, while Sylvinet was still a pretty boy, paler and more slender than his brother. So, they were no longer mistaken for each other, and though they still looked like brothers, no one took them for twins at first sight. Landry, who was born an hour after Sylvinet, and on that account was called the younger, impressed strangers as being a year or two the elder. So Father Barbeau's preference for him became more and more marked; for, like most country people, he valued strength and size above everything.

XI

❦

Chapter 11

For a short time after Landry's adventure with little Fadette, the boy worried a good deal about the promise he had made her. At the time when she had relieved his anxiety, he would willingly have pledged himself that his father and mother would give her a choice of anything the Twinnery contained. But when he saw that Father Barbeau had not taken Sylvinet's fit of the sulks so very much to heart, he was afraid that when little Fadette came to claim her reward, his father might shut the door in her face, and ridicule her pretensions and the fine promise which Landry had made her. Landry was very much mortified at this idea, and as his trouble wore off, it seemed to him that he had been very silly to fancy that there was anything of the supernatural in the occurrences of that afternoon. He was suspicious that little Fadette had been making a fool of him, though there might be some doubt on that subject, and he could think of no good reasons to give his father by way of proving to him that he had acted wisely in making an agreement which entailed such serious consequences. On the other hand, it did not seem possible to break the contract; for he had pledged his word in perfect honour and sincerity. But, to his great surprise, neither the day following his adventure, nor that month, nor during the whole season, did he hear anything about little Fadette at the Twinnery or at La Priche. She did not come to Father Caillaud's and ask to see Landry, nor did she go to Father Barbeau's to put in her claim, and when Landry got a distant view of her in the fields she did not come to meet him, and never took any notice of him, which was quite unlike her; for she was in the habit of running after everybody, staring at them inquisitively, laughing, joking, and chaffing with those who were in a good humour, or scoffing and jeering at those who were not. But as Mother Fadet lived about half-way between La Priche and La Cosse, Landry would be certain to meet little Fadette someday, face to face, in the road; and when the road is rather narrow, you cannot well avoid giving some sort of a greeting as you pass by.

So one evening as little Fadette was bringing home her geese—her Grasshopper at her heels, as usual—and Landry, who had been to the meadow after his mares, was driving them quietly along toward La Priche, they met in the little road which leads down from the Cross of the Bossons to the Roulettes ford, and which is so sunken between two embankments that there was no escape. Landry coloured, afraid that he would be called upon to keep his promise, and wishing to discourage Fadette, he jumped on one of the mares the moment he caught sight of her, and kicked the animal's sides with his sabots to make her trot.

But as all the mares were hobbled, the one he was riding could not go any faster. Landry, seeing that Fadette was close at hand, did not dare to look at her, and turned around, pretending to see if his colts were following him. When he looked ahead again, Fadette had already passed him, without saying a word. He could not even tell whether she had looked at him, or tried to give him a goodnight smile. He saw only Jeanet, the Grasshopper, who—as impish and hateful as ever—picked up a stone to throw at his mare's legs. Landry felt like giving him a cut with his whip, but he dreaded having to stop and explain matters with the sister. So, he pretended not to see him and rode on without looking back.

The same thing happened whenever he met Fadette. By degrees he plucked up courage to look her in the face; for as he grew older and wiser, he did not attach so much importance to so trifling an affair. But when he tried to catch her eye, to show her that he was ready to listen to anything she might have to say, he was surprised to see that the girl purposely turned her head in the other direction, as if she were as much afraid of him as he was of her. This discovery increased his confidence, and, as he was disposed to give everyone his due, it occurred to him that he had done very wrong never to have thanked her for the pleasure she had given him, whether it was by chance or owing to her superior knowledge.

He made up his mind to speak to her the first time he saw her, and when the opportunity occurred, he advanced at least ten steps toward her, intending to say how do you do, and have a little chat.

But as he approached, little Fadette was very much on her

dignity, and when she finally made up her mind to speak to him, her manner was so disdainful that he was quite taken aback, and did not dare say a word to her. Landry did not speak to her again that year; for, from that day on, little Fadette, from some caprice or other, took so much trouble to avoid him that when she saw him coming, she would turn aside into some field, or go a long distance out of her way, so that she might not meet him. Landry thought she was angry at his ingratitude, but he could not bear to make the first advances. Little Fadette was not like other children. She was not naturally ready to take offence; indeed, she was not enough so, for she loved to tease, and her tongue was so sharp that she was very quick at repartee, and always managed to have the last word. She had never been known to sulk, and people even accused her of being lacking in that proper pride which a girl should have when she gets to be fifteen and begins to think herself of some consequence. She was full of boyish pranks, and often tried to tease Sylvinet; she would bother him and try to provoke him, and make him lose his temper, when she caught him in a brown study, for he still indulged in occasional daydreams. She always ran after him part of the way when she met him—ridiculing him for being a twin, and tormenting him by saying that Landry did not love him, and only laughed at his woes. So poor Sylvinet, who had much more confidence in her powers of witchcraft than Landry had, was amazed that she had guessed his thoughts and hated her with all his heart. He despised her and her family, and he avoided the hateful Cricket just as she avoided Landry; for, said he, sooner or later she will follow her mother's example. The latter had been a woman of bad character and had finally left her husband and gone off as a camp follower. She had gone to be a *vivandière* soon after the Grasshopper was born, and had never been heard of since. Her husband had died of grief and shame, and so old Mother Fadet was obliged to take charge of the two children, who fared very badly, as much on account of her stinginess as from her advanced age, which rendered her unfit to look after them and see that they were properly brought up.

For all these reasons, Landry, though he was not so proud as Sylvinet, felt disgust for little Fadette, and, regretting that he had ever had anything to do with her, was careful not to let anybody know of it. He did not even tell his twin, not wishing him to know how anxious he had been on his account. Sylvinet, on the other hand, said nothing about little Fadette's tormenting him, being ashamed to tell that she had found out how jealous he was.

But time did not stand still. Weeks are like months, and months like years with youngsters the age of our twins; so far, at least, as concerns the changes they work in mind and body. Landry soon forgot his adventure, and, after worrying himself a little about Fadette, gave no more thought to the affair than if it had been a dream.

Landry had been at La Priche about ten months, and St. John's Day—the period when his engagement with Father Caillaud would expire—was close at hand. That honest man was so pleased with him that he had determined to raise his wages, sooner than let him go. And Landry asked nothing better than to remain near his family and renew his engagement with the La Priche folks, to whom he was much attached. Besides that, he had taken a fancy to a niece of Father Caillaud's, named Madelon, who was a fine slip of a girl. She was a year older than he, and still looked upon him as a child, but less and less so every day. At the beginning of the year, she had made fun of him because he was ashamed to kiss her in their dances or games, but latterly, she had taken to blushing instead of teasing him and avoided being alone with him in the stable or hayloft. Madelon was pretty well off, and a marriage might very well have been arranged between them, in the course of time. Both families were much esteemed in that part of the country. Finally, Father Caillaud, noticing that these youngsters were fond of each other's society, but yet dreaded to be left alone together, told Father Barbeau that they would make a fine couple and that there would be no harm in allowing them to become better acquainted.

So, a week before St. John's Day, it was agreed that Landry should remain at La Priche, and that Sylvinet should not leave home; for he was a very sensible young fellow now, and as Father Barbeau had had an intermittent fever, he found him very useful about the farm. Sylvinet dreaded being sent far away, and this dread had a good effect on him; for he tried more and more to overcome his excessive fondness for Landry, or, at least, not to allow it to be so evident. So, peace and contentment had returned to the Twinnery, though the twins did not see each other oftener than once or twice a week.

The feast of St. John was a happy day for them; they all went to town to see the hiring out of servants for the city and country, and the festival which followed, on the public square. Landry danced the bourrée more than once with Madelon, and, to please him, Sylvinet tried to dance too. He did not make out very well,

but Madelon was very good to him, and when she was dancing opposite him, she took his hand to show him the step. So
Sylvinet, only too glad to be with his brother, promised to learn
to dance well, so as to share an enjoyment which he had hitherto
begrudged Landry.

He was not particularly jealous of Madelon, for Landry did
not, as yet, pay her very devoted attention. Besides that, Madelon flattered Sylvinet and encouraged him. She was quite at her
ease with him, and those who knew no better would have supposed that she preferred him to his brother. Landry might have
found some occasion for jealousy, but it was not in his nature to
feel jealous of anybody, and perhaps, in spite of his innocence, he
had a slight suspicion that Madelon only behaved thus to please
him, and to make opportunities of seeing him more frequently.

So, for about three months everything went on smoothly, till
the feast of St. Andoche—the patron saint of La Cosse—which
is about the last of September. This day—which had always been
a special holiday for the twins, because there were games and
dancing under the walnut trees in the village—this year brought
them new and unexpected troubles.

Father Caillaud, having given Landry permission the night
before to go and sleep at the Twinnery, so that he might take
part in the early morning festivities, Landry started off before
supper, delighted with the idea of taking his twin by surprise; for
he was not expected till the next day. The days were beginning
to shorten, and it grew dark early. Landry was afraid of nothing
in broad daylight, but it would not have been natural, at his age
and in his part of the country, if he had enjoyed being alone on
the roads after nightfall, especially in the autumn, which is the

season when witches and will-o'-the-wisps begin to hold their revels, on account of the fogs which help them to hide their naughty pranks and misdemeanours. Landry, who was used to going about alone at all hours, driving his oxen to and fro, was not more timid that evening than any other, but he walked fast and sang at the top of his voice; for, as everybody knows, a man's singing scares away evil-disposed people as well as prowling beasts.

When he reached the Roulettes ford—so called on account of the round pebbles which abound there—he turned up the bottom of his trousers, for fear that the water might be above his ankles, and was careful not to walk straight ahead; for the ford runs obliquely, and there are some dangerous holes to the right and left of it. Landry had so often crossed the ford and was so familiar with it, that he could not make a mistake. Besides, from where he was standing, he could see, through the trees, which were half stripped of their leaves, the little light which came from Mother Fadet's house, and by keeping his eyes on that light, and walking straight towards it, there was no danger of making a misstep.

It was so dark under the trees, however, that Landry sounded the ford with his stick before stepping in. He was surprised to find that the water was deeper than usual, though he could hear the noise from the sluice gates, which had been open fully an hour. However, as he could see the light in Fadette's window, he ventured in, but, after a step or two, he found himself in water up to his knees, and drew back, thinking that he must have made a mistake. He tried it a little higher up, and a little lower down, but he found the water even deeper in both places. There had been no rain, and the sluice gates were still open, for he could hear the rushing of the water. It was very strange.

XII

⊱❈⊰

Chapter 12

"I must have tried to cross at the wrong place," thought Landry; "for all of a sudden, I see Fadette's candle on my right, and it should be on my left." He went up the road as far as the Croix-aux-Lièvres (the Hare's Cross) and walked around it with his eyes shut, so as to put himself straight, and, after taking a good look at the surrounding trees and bushes, he struck the right road and returned to the river. But though the ford seemed all right, he did not venture to go forward more than a step or two, for all at once he saw just behind him the light from Fadette's house, which should be directly in front. He returned to the bank, and now the light seemed to be in its usual place. He tried the ford again, cutting across in another direction, and this time the water came nearly up to his waist. Nevertheless, he kept on, thinking that he must have stepped into a hole, but that he would get out again if he walked straight toward the light.

He was obliged to stop; for the hole was getting deeper and deeper, and the water was now up to his shoulders. It felt very cold, and he paused a moment to consider whether he should retrace his steps; for the light seemed to have changed its position, and he could even see it move, flit along, leap and skip from one bank to the other, and finally he saw it reflected in the water, where it hovered like a bird, poising itself on its wings, and making a faint sputtering noise like a resinous torch.

By this time Landry was really very much frightened, and he had heard it said that there is nothing more dangerous and misleading than that very fire. He had been told that it took delight in leading astray those who looked at it and would lure them into the very deepest part of the water, laughing at them, after a fashion of its own, and mocking at its victims in their despair.

Landry shut his eyes, to avoid seeing it, and, turning quickly round, he waded out of the hole at all risks, and found his way back to the shore. Then he threw himself down on the grass and stared at the will-o'-the-wisp, which continued its dance, still mocking him. It was indeed a weird, uncanny sight. Sometimes it darted about like a kingfisher, and sometimes it vanished altogether. Again, it looked as big as a bull's head, and then, in a twinkling, it was no larger than a cat's eye. It came close to Landry, then whirled about him so fast that it dazzled him, and finally, seeing that he would not follow, it fluttered back among the rushes and lay there sulking, as if planning some new insult.

Landry dared not stir, for he could not rid himself of the will-o'-the-wisp by retracing his steps. Everybody knows how it persists in pursuing those who try to run away from it, and keeps on crossing their path, till they go mad, and tumble into some snare or other.

He sat there shivering with fear and cold, when he heard, just behind him, a thin little voice, singing:

"Fay, fay, my little fay,
Take thy torch, and haste away,
Here's my cap, and here's my cloak,
And here's a mate for fairy folk."

And the next moment, little Fadette, who was gayly preparing to cross the stream, apparently not the least bit afraid or astonished at the sight of the Jack-o'-lantern, stumbled over Landry, who was sitting on the ground in the darkness, and drew back, swearing like a boy, and that, too, not as if it were the first time.

"Don't you know me, Fanchon? Don't be afraid. I am not an enemy of yours." He said this because he was almost as much afraid of her as he was of the will-o'-the-wisp. He had heard her song and knew well enough that it was a spell to charm the will-o'-the-wisp, which danced and spun around in front of her, like a mad thing, as if in token of welcome.

"I know very well, my pretty twin," said little Fadette, after a moment's reflection, "that you only speak kindly to me because you are half dead of fright, and your voice is as shaky as my grandmother's. So, faint heart, you are not so proud at night as you are in the daytime, and I'll wager you dare not cross the stream without me."

"As sure as I live," said Landry, "I have just come out of it, and I narrowly escaped drowning. Will you venture in, Fadette? Do you think you can find the ford?"

"Why not, I'd like to know? But I see what is worrying you," answered little Fadette, laughing. "Come, give me your hand, coward! The will-o'-the-wisp is not so bad as you think, and it never hurts those who are not afraid of it. I am used to it, and we are old acquaintances."

Then, with more strength than Landry had given her credit for possessing, she took him by the arm, and pulled him toward the ford at a run, singing as she went,

"I'll take my cape and haste away, for every fairy has her fay."

Landry felt hardly more at ease in the society of the little witch than in that of the will-o'-the-wisp. As, however, he found the devil less alarming in the form of a human being than in that of such a flickering, treacherous flame, he made no resistance and was soon quite reassured when he found that Fadette was guiding him so well that he walked dry-footed over the pebbles. But as they went rather rapidly, they made a current of air for the will-o'-the-wisp; and they were followed up quite closely by this meteor, as our schoolmaster calls it, and he seems to know all about it, and says that we have no reason to be afraid of it.

XIII

❦

Chapter 13

It may be that Mother Fadet had some knowledge on the subject too, and had taught her granddaughter not to be afraid of these fires which are only seen at night, or perhaps, having seen so many of them—for they are very frequent in the neighbourhood of the Roulettes ford, and it was a wonder that Landry had never before seen one near at hand—the little girl had come to the conclusion that they did not originate from an evil source and would do her no harm. Feeling Landry tremble from head to foot as the will-o'-the-wisp approached them, she said, "You silly boy, that fire won't burn, and if you were nimble enough to catch it, you'd find that it doesn't even leave a mark."

"So much the worse," thought Landry; "I know what kind of fire it is which won't burn. It isn't the kind of fire that God makes, for God's fire is intended to burn and give heat."

But he kept his thoughts to himself, and when he stood on

the bank, safe and sound, he had a great mind to leave her there, and hurry off to the Twinnery. But he was not ungrateful at heart, and so did not like to start off without a word of thanks.

"This is the second time you have done me a service, Fanchon Fadet," said he, "and I should be too mean for anything if I didn't tell you that I shall never forget it as long as I live. I was sitting there like a fool when you found me. The will-o'-the-wisp had cast a spell over me, and I could not move. I should never have crossed the river, or rather I should never have got out of it."

Perhaps you could have crossed with neither trouble nor danger if you had not been so foolish," answered Fadette. "I never would have believed that a big boy like you, in his seventeenth year, and who will soon have a beard on his chin, could be so easily scared, and I am glad I saw you."

"And why are you glad, Fanchon Fadet?"

"Because I don't like you," said she disdainfully.

"And why don't you like me?"

"Because I have a very poor opinion of you; you and your twin and your father and mother, who are proud because they are rich, and who think that you are doing nothing but your duty when you do them a service. They have taught you to be ungrateful, Landry, and that is the worst fault a man can have except being a coward."

Landry was much humiliated by the little girl's reproaches, for he was quite aware that they were not altogether undeserved; and he said to her, "If I am to blame, Fadette, it is nobody's fault but my own. Neither my brother, my father, my mother, nor any of my friends know of the help you gave me once before. But this time they shall know of it, and you shall have any reward you please."

"Ah, how proud you are," answered little Fadette, "because you think that you can get even with me by giving me presents. You think that I am like my grandmother, who lets people abuse and insult her as much as they please, so long as they give her a little money. I don't want any of your presents, let me tell you, and I despise anything you could give me because you have never had the decency to say a single word of thanks or kindness to me since that time last year when I helped you out of a great trouble."

"I am to blame, I acknowledge, Fadette," said Landry, who could not help feeling astonished to hear her, for the first time, talk so sensibly. "But it is also a little your fault. You didn't need to use much magic to find my brother when you had, no doubt, just seen him, while I was talking to your grandmother. If you really had a kind heart—you who accuse me of having none at all—instead of keeping me waiting when I was so anxious, and instead of giving me directions which might have misled me, you would have told me at once, 'Go to the meadow and you will find him there on the bank of the river.' That would have been easy enough for you to do, instead of amusing yourself at my expense—that is the reason I have not attached so much value to the service you did me."

Little Fadette, who was usually quick at repartee, stopped to think a moment. Then said she: "It is very plain that you have done your best to banish gratitude from your heart, and to make yourself believe that you owe me nothing because of the reward which I made you promise me. But—I tell you again—you have a bad heart since it has not told you that I have never asked you for anything, and have not even reproached you for your ingratitude."

"That's true, Fadette," said Landry, who was truth itself; "I have done wrong. I knew it and was ashamed of it. I should have spoken to you. I did intend to, but you looked at me so savagely that I didn't know how to go about it."

"If you had come and spoken a kind word to me the day after that affair, you would not have found me savage; you would have seen at once that I did not want to be paid, and we should have made friends with each other. Instead of that, I have just now a very poor opinion of you, and I ought to have left you to fight it out with the will-o'-the-wisp as well as you could. Goodnight, Landry of the Twinnery; go and dry your clothes; go and tell your parents, if it had not been for that ragged little wretch of a Cricket, I should have drunk my fill of the river tonight, as sure as I am alive." And as she spoke, little Fadette turned her back on him and walked off toward her house, singing:

"Take your lesson then, and go,
My pretty twin, Landry Barbeau."

By this time Landry felt very repentant, not that he was disposed to be friends with a girl who seemed to have more wit than kindliness, and whose rude manners did not attract even those who found them amusing, but he was a lad of good principles, and he liked to have a clear conscience. He ran after her and caught hold of her cape.

"See here, Fanchon Fadet!" said he, "we must settle this affair between us and be done with it. You are angry with me, and I am not over well pleased with myself. You must tell me what you want, and I will bring it to you not later than tomorrow."

"I never want to see you again," answered Fadette, harshly. "No matter what you bring me, you may depend upon it, I shall throw it in your face."

"That's a hard way to talk to a person who is trying to make amends to you. If you don't want a present, perhaps there is something I can do for you to show you that I wish you no harm. Come, tell me what I can do to satisfy you!"

"Then you are not going to ask my pardon, and try to make friends with me?" said Fadette, standing still.

"Ask your pardon? That's pretty hard," answered Landry, who did not fancy the notion of apologizing to a girl who was not in the habit of receiving the consideration to which her age entitled her, and who did not always behave herself with the greatest propriety. "As for your friendship, Fadette, you have such a queer disposition that I shouldn't trust you very far. So, ask for something which I can give you outright, and shall not be obliged to take back again."

"Well," said Fadette, in a clear, cold voice, "it shall be as you wish, Landry, the twin. I have offered you my forgiveness and you won't accept it. Now I claim the promise you made me, which was, to obey my orders whenever I should call upon you. That will be tomorrow, the feast of St. Andoche, and this is what I want you to do. You must dance the bourrée with me three times after Mass, twice after Vespers, and twice more after the Angelus: that makes seven times. And all day long, from the time you get up till you go to bed, you shall not dance the bourrée with anybody else—girl or married woman. If you don't do it, I shall know that you have three very ugly traits in your disposition: you are a coward, you are ungrateful, and you do not keep your word. Goodnight; I'll wait for you at the church tomorrow, to open the dance."

And little Fadette, whom Landry had followed to her house, drew the bolt and went in so quickly that the door was shut and bolted before the twin had a chance to say a word in reply.

XIV

❦

Chapter 14

At first Landry thought Fadette's idea so amusing that he was more inclined to laugh than to be annoyed.

"There is a girl," said he to himself, "who is more foolish than malicious, and more disinterested than one would suppose; for it won't ruin my family to give her her reward." But, on second thoughts, the payment of his debt seemed more difficult than he had been inclined to think it at first. Little Fadette danced very well; he had seen her skipping about the fields and road with the shepherd lads, and she flew about like a little demon, so quickly that her partner could hardly keep up with her. But she was so far from pretty and so badly dressed, even on Sundays, that no boy of Landry's age would ever have thought of asking her to dance—especially in public. It was as much as could be expected if the swineherds and the boys who had not yet made their first communion should condescend to ask her, and the country belles did not like to have her dance in the same set with them. So, Landry felt very much mortified at having engaged himself to such a partner, and when he recollected that he had asked pretty Madelon to dance at least three bourrées with him, he wondered how she would take the affront which he should be obliged to offer her, by failing to claim the dances.

As he was cold and hungry, and was still afraid that the will-o'-the-wisp might follow him, he hurried along, not thinking much about anything, and never once looking behind him. As soon as he got home, he dried his clothes and told his parents that he could not find the ford, on account of the darkness, and the trouble he had had in getting across the river. But he was ashamed to tell how frightened he had been, and he said nothing about little Fadette or the will-o'-the-wisp. He went to bed, saying to himself that tomorrow would be soon enough to bother himself about the consequences of this unlucky adventure. But, try as he would, he slept very badly. He dreamed more than fifty times that he saw little Fadette mounted astride of the goblin, which looked like a big red rooster, and which held in one claw its horn lantern with a candle in it, which lighted up the whole rush field. And then little Fadette was changed into a cricket as big as a goat, and shouted out to him, in a voice like a cricket, a song which he could not understand, but of which he caught now and then some words which rhymed, such as, "fay, way, cloak, folk," etc. His head was splitting with the noise, and the will-o'-the-wisp's light was so vivid, and flickered so much, that when he woke up his eyes were still dazzled and saw those little black, red, and blue balls which float before them when we have been looking too steadily at the sun or moon.

Landry was so worn out with his bad night, that he slept all through Mass, and did not hear one word of the Curé's sermon, which was a eulogy on the virtues and general character of good St. Andoche. On coming out of church, Landry was so drowsy that he forgot all about Fadette. But there she stood, in front of the porch, next to pretty Madelon, who had stationed herself there, quite confident that the first invitation would be for her. But when he approached to speak to her, he could not help seeing the Cricket, who stepped forward and said in a loud voice and with unparalleled impudence, "See here, Landry, you asked me last night to give you the first dance, and I depend on you to see that we don't miss it!"

Landry turned as red as fire, and seeing that Madelon coloured too, with astonishment and displeasure at such an unheard of occurrence, he mustered up courage to say to Fadette, "I may have promised to give you a dance, Cricket, but I had asked someone else before you, and your turn will come after I have kept my previous engagement."

"No, indeed," said Fadette, boldly. "Your memory fails you, Landry. You haven't a previous engagement with anybody, for I claim a promise you made me last year, and which you renewed only last evening. If Madelon wants to dance with you today, here is your twin, who is so like you that he can take your place. One is as good as the other."

"The Cricket is right," said Madelon, haughtily, taking Sylvinet's hand. "Since you have an engagement of such long standing, you must keep it, Landry—I would just as soon dance with your brother."

"Yes, yes, it is all the same thing," said Sylvinet, innocently. "We can all four dance together."

Landry had to let it pass, for he did not want to attract people's attention, and the Cricket began to skip about with such pride and agility that no bourrée was ever danced with more spirit and in better time. If she had been pretty and attractive, it would have been a pleasure to look at her; for she danced wonderfully well, and there was not a pretty girl present who would not have been glad to have her ease and lightness. But the poor Cricket was so badly dressed that she looked ten times uglier than usual. Landry dared not look at Madelon, for he felt deeply mortified at being obliged to treat her as he had done; so, he watched his partner, and thought her even uglier than in her everyday rags. She had tried to deck herself out in holiday attire and the result was absurd.

She wore a cap which had grown yellow with lying away, and instead of being small and well caught-up behind, as the country girls wear them nowadays, it had two great ears on either side of her head, and, at the back, the cape falling down on her neck made her look like her grandmother, and gave her a head as big as a bushel basket, on her slender, little stick of a neck. Her coarse woollen petticoat was two hands-breadths too short, and as she had grown a good deal the past year, her thin, sunburnt arms protruded from her sleeves like spider's legs. She wore a crimson apron, of which she was very proud. It had been her mother's, and she had not thought to take off the bib, though they had not been worn by young girls these ten years or more.

She was not very coquettish, poor girl; indeed, she was not enough so, and had grown up like a boy, never thinking of her appearance, and caring for nothing but fun and play. She looked like an old woman in her Sunday clothes, and was laughed at for her shabby get-up, which was the result of the grandmother's stinginess and the granddaughter's lack of taste, and not of poverty.

XV

Chapter 15

Sylvinet thought it odd that his twin should have taken such a fancy to Fadette, for whom his own dislike was even greater than Landry's had been. Landry could not explain matters and felt as if he should sink through the ground. Madelon was very indignant, and in spite of the nimble time which Fadette made them keep, their faces were as gloomy as if they had been at a funeral. At the end of the first dance, Landry slipped away to try to hide in his orchard. But in a moment, little Fadette, escorted by the Grasshopper—who was more quarrelsome and noisy than ever, because he had a peacock's feather and a new gilt tassel on his cap—came to hunt him up, followed by a troop of impish little girls—younger than herself; for girls of her own age would not have anything to do with her. When Landry saw her coming with all this crew, who were to be her witnesses in case of a refusal to go with her, he gave in at once, and led her out under the walnut trees, looking about for a corner where they could dance without attracting so much attention.

Fortunately for him, Madelon and Sylvinet had gone off somewhere else, and there were none of his neighbours about; so he took advantage of the opportunity to dance his third dance with Fadette. There were none but strangers near, who paid very little attention to them.

As soon as he was through dancing, he ran to find Madelon to invite her to go out under the trees and eat some frumenty with him. But she had been dancing with other young men, who had made her promise to allow them to treat her, and she refused, rather haughtily. Then noticing that he stood in a corner, with his eyes full of tears—for pride and anger had made her prettier than ever, and it seemed to him as if everybody must notice it—she ate very fast, rose from the table, and said aloud:

"There goes Vespers. Whom am I going to dance with afterwards?" She turned toward Landry, expecting him to say at once, "With me!" But, before he could open his mouth, other young men presented themselves, and Madelon, not deigning to vouchsafe him one look of pity or reproach, went off to Vespers with her new admirers.

When Vespers was over, Madelon started off with Pierre Aubardeau, followed by Jean Aladenise and Etienne Alaphilippe, and danced with all three, one after the other; for she was too pretty a girl to lack partners, especially as she had a nice little fortune of her own.

Landry stood looking after her out of the corners of his eyes, and little Fadette had remained in church after the others were gone, saying some long prayers. She did this every Sunday, some said because she was so pious, and others because she wished to disguise her dealings with the devil.

Landry was very sorry to see that Madelon did not seem at all concerned about him, that her face was rosy with enjoyment, and that she no longer appeared to feel the affront which he had been compelled to offer her. He had not thought of it before, but it now occurred to him that she must be something of a coquette, and that, at any rate, she could not care much for him, since she managed to enjoy herself so well without him. It is true that appearances were against him; but she had seen how distressed he was when they were out under the walnut trees, and she might have known that there must be something behind, which he wanted an opportunity to explain to her. But she never gave him a thought, and was as frisky as a young kid, while his own heart was bursting with grief.

After she had finished dancing with her three partners, Landry went up to her, wishing to have a few words with her in private, so that he might make some attempt to clear himself. He did not know how he should manage to draw her aside—for he was still too young to be at his ease with women—and as he could not think of the proper thing to say, he took her hand to lead her apart, but she said to him, half petulant and half relenting: "Well, Landry, have you come to ask me to dance at last?"

"Not to dance," said he, for he did not know how to act a part, and had no intention of breaking his word; "but to tell you something which you cannot refuse to hear."

"Oh, if you have a secret to tell me, Landry, you must keep it till another time," answered Madelon, drawing away her hand. "Today is a day for dancing and merrymaking. I am not tired out yet, and if the Cricket has danced you down, go home, and go to bed if you want to—I am going to stay."

Thereupon she accepted the invitation of Germain Audoux, who came up to ask her to dance. And as she turned her back, Landry heard Germain Audoux say to her, speaking of him: "That boy seems to think that this dance belongs to him."

"Maybe he does," said Madelon, tossing her head; "but I shan't give it to any such fellow as he is."

Landry was much shocked at this expression and lingered near to watch Madelon's behaviour, which, while not absolutely rude, was so proud and haughty that it made him angry. And when she came near him again, and he looked at her rather disdainfully, she said to him, out of bravado: "Well, Landry, so you can't find a partner today? As sure as I live, you will be obliged to go back to the Cricket."

"I'll go back to her gladly enough," answered Landry, "for if she isn't the prettiest girl here, she is the best dancer."

Then off he went to hunt through the church for little Fadette, and brought her back to the dance, right opposite to Madelon, and danced two bourrées with her without stopping. It was worth something to see how proud and happy the Cricket was. She did not attempt to conceal her delight; snapped her merry black eyes, and tossed her head with its great cap, like a chicken with a topknot.

But, unfortunately, her triumph gave umbrage to five or six little ragamuffins who had been in the habit of dancing with her. They had never looked down on her but had always admired her dancing, and now when they found that they couldn't get near her, they fell to criticising her, calling her proud, and whispering so that she could hear them: "Just look at the Cricket! She thinks she can charm Landry Barbeau!" Cricket, Grasshopper, singed cat, little runt, will-o'-the-wisp, and many other nicknames popular among country people.

XVI

Chapter 16

And then when little Fadette was dancing near them, they would pull her sleeve or put out a foot to trip her up, and there were some of them—the youngest ones, of course, and the most unmannerly—who struck at the ears of her cap, and tilted it first to one side and then to the other, shouting, " Three cheers for the big helmet! Mother Fadet's big helmet!"

The poor Cricket struck out at them five or six times, aiming her blows to the right and left, but that only served to draw attention to herself, and the neighbours began to say: "Just look at our Cricket! What luck she's having today! Landry Barbeau dances with her all the time. She dances well, to be sure, but she is putting on fine lady airs and strutting about like a magpie."

Some of them said to Landry: "Poor Landry! Has she bewitched you so that you can't look at anybody else? Or maybe she is going to teach you the black art, and we'll soon see you driving the wolves to pasture."

Landry was mortified, but Sylvinet, who admired his brother beyond anything in the world, was still more ashamed when he saw him make a laughing-stock of himself before so many people, many of them strangers, who now began to take an interest in the affair, asking questions and saying: "That's a fine-looking boy, but it is queer that he should take up with the ugliest girl here."

Madelon came up to listen triumphantly to these jeers and took part in them with great relish. She said: "What can you expect? Landry is nothing but a child, and boys of his age don't care whether a girl has a goat's head or a human face, as long as they can get her to talk to them."

Sylvinet took Landry by the arm and said to him in a low voice: "Come, brother, let's go home, or we'll have to take some notice of them, for they are making fun of you, and it reflects on you when they insult little Fadette. I can't imagine what put it into your head to dance with her five or six times running. It seems as if you were trying to make yourself ridiculous. Do stop amusing yourself after such a fashion, I beg of you. It's all right for her to expose herself to being laughed at by the crowd if she chooses to do it; she likes that sort of thing: it just suits her. But it doesn't suit us. Let's go. We'll come back after the Angelus, and you can dance with Madelon, who is a very well-behaved girl. I've always told you that you were too fond of dancing and that your love for it will make a fool of you yet."

Landry followed him a step or two, but he turned back when he heard a great clatter of voices, and saw that Madelon and the other girls had given little Fadette over to the rough horse-play of their sweethearts and that the little vagabonds—encouraged by the laughter which greeted their efforts—had just knocked off her cap. Her long black hair streamed down her back and she was defending herself frantically, in a perfect frenzy of indignation. For once in her lifetime she had done nothing to provoke such ill-treatment. She was crying with rage, and could not recover her cap, which a naughty little rascal had carried off on the end of a stick.

Landry was disgusted with the whole affair and —angry at seeing her so unjustly treated—he rescued the cap, and gave the boy a sound thrashing with the stick. Then he turned his attention to the others, who scattered in every direction as soon as they saw him coming, and, taking the poor Cricket by the hand, he gave her back her cap.

Landry's energetic proceedings, and the terror of the little ragamuffins, greatly amused the spectators. They applauded Landry, but as he was not in Madelon's good graces, some of the boys of his own age, and even older, were rather disposed to laugh at his expense.

Landry no longer felt ashamed. He was conscious of his own strength and courage, and a certain feeling of manliness assured him that he was doing his duty in defending any woman—pretty or ugly, big or little—whom he had taken for a partner in the presence of his friends and neighbours. He noticed that Madelon's party was inclined to make fun of him, so he walked straight up to the Aladenises and the Alaphilippes, and said to them: "Well, fellows, what have you got to say to me? If I see fit to pay attention to that girl, what business is it of yours? If you don't like it, why don't you speak out? Can't you see me standing here before you? Somebody said I was only a child, but there isn't a man here, or even a big boy, who would dare say it to my face. Come, speak up! We'll see if anybody is going to interfere with the girl who has been dancing with a child like me!"

Sylvinet stood by his brother's side, and though he had opposed getting into this quarrel, he was ready to back him up. There were four or five of the young men who were a head taller than the twins, but when they saw them so determined and were themselves of the opinion that it was not worthwhile to fight about so small a matter, they did not say a word but exchanged glances as if asking who wanted to have it out with Landry. No one came forward, and Landry, who still held Fadette's hand, said to her: "Quick—put on your cap, Fadette, and let's dance, and we'll see if anybody will try to take it off."

"No," said little Fadette, drying her tears; "I have danced enough for today, and I will not hold you to the rest."

"No, no; we must dance again," said Landry, who was all afire with pride and courage. "Nobody shall say that you can't dance with me without being insulted."

So, he made her dance again, and nobody said a word to him, or even looked askance. Madelon and her admirers had taken themselves off to dance somewhere else. After the bourrée was over, little Fadette said to Landry in a low tone: "Now that's enough, Landry. I am satisfied with you, and I let you off your promise. I am going home. Dance with whom you please this evening."

And off she ran after her brother, who had been fighting with the other children, and was gone before Landry saw which way she took.

XVII

Chapter 17

Landry went home to supper with his brother, and as Sylvinet was very much disturbed over the morning's occurrences, he told him how he had met the will-o'-the-wisp the night before, and how little Fadette had helped him out of his difficulty, either by her courage or by some little piece of witchcraft, and had asked, as her reward, that he should dance with her seven times at the feast of St. Andoche.

He did not tell him the rest, not wishing him to know how he had feared to find him drowned in the river the year before. In this he showed his good sense; for the bad notions children take into their heads are very apt to return, if people take notice of them, or talk to them on the subject. Sylvinet thought that his brother had done right to keep his word, and told him that he respected him all the more on account of the annoyance it had cost him. But while realizing the danger Landry had been in, he did not feel grateful to little Fadette. He disliked her so much that he would not believe that her presence there was accidental, nor that her assistance had been given from kindly motives.

"She must have conjured up the will-o'-the-wisp to confuse you and get you drowned. But God would not permit it, because you are not, and have never been, in a state of mortal sin. Then that wicked Cricket, taking advantage of your gratitude and kindness of heart, got you to make her a promise which she knew would be very annoying and injurious to you. She is terribly malicious, that girl. All witches love to do all the mischief they can, and there is no such thing as a good witch. She knew well enough that she would get you into trouble with Madelon and all the most respectable of your acquaintances. She tried to get you into a fight, too. And if the good Lord had not protected you against her for the second time, you might have got into some very serious dispute and have been hurt."

Landry, who had a habit of seeing everything through his brother's eyes, thought that he was probably right, and did not try to defend Fadette. They talked about the will-o'-the-wisp, which Sylvinet had never seen, and which he was very curious to hear about, though he had not the least desire to see it. But they did not dare speak of it to their mother, for she was alarmed at the very thought of it; nor to their father, because he laughed at it, and had seen it more than twenty times, without paying any attention to it. The dancing was kept up till very late, but Landry, who was very low-spirited on account of his falling out with Madelon, would not take advantage of the freedom which Fadette had allowed him, and went off with his brother to bring the cattle home from pasture. And as he was halfway back to La

Priche, and had a headache, he bade his brother goodnight at the end of the rush field. Sylvinet would not let him cross the Roulettes ford, for fear that the will-o'-the-wisp or the Cricket might play him some ill turn. He made him promise to take the longest way and to cross the footbridge by the big mill. Landry did as his brother told him, and instead of crossing the rush field, he took the road which runs at the foot of Chaumois Hill.

He did not feel at all timid, for the sounds of merrymaking were still in the air. He could catch the faint, distant notes of the bagpipes, and the shouts of the dancers at the feast of St. Andoche, and he well knew that evil spirits do not play their pranks till everybody in the neighbourhood is asleep. When he reached the foot of the hill, he heard somebody sobbing and crying beside the road, and thought at first that it was a curlew. But as he drew near, it sounded like a human voice, and as his heart never failed him when he had to do with a fellow being, especially if in need of assistance, he leapt down into the hollow beside the road, without a moment's hesitation. But the sobs ceased as he approached.

"Who is crying here?" asked he, in a loud voice.

No answer.

"Is anybody ill?" and as there was still no reply, he was about to go away, when he thought he would take a look among the stones and brambles which obstructed the place, and he soon saw by the light of the moon, which was just rising, someone lying on the ground, at full length, face downward and as motionless as a dead body. He could not tell whether the person was really dead, or whether he had thrown himself down there in great distress, and would not stir for fear of being seen.

Landry had never seen or touched a corpse, and was quite overcome at the notion that this might be one; but he controlled his fears because he knew that it was his duty to help his neighbour and walked resolutely up to take the hand of the prostrate figure, which half rose as soon as it became evident that disguise was no longer possible, and Landry recognized little Fadette.

XVIII

⥽⥼

Chapter 18

At first, Landry was annoyed to find little Fadette again in his way, but as she appeared to be in trouble, he felt sorry for her. This is the conversation which ensued between them.

"What, Cricket! Was that you crying like that? Has anybody hurt you, or run after you, that you have hidden here to cry?"

" No, Landry, nobody has bothered me since you defended me so bravely, and besides that, I am not afraid of anybody. I hid myself to cry, that's all; for there's nothing so silly as to let other people see you when you are in trouble."

"But why are you in such great trouble? Is it because they were so rude to you today? It was partly your own fault, but you must cheer up and never expose yourself to such treatment again."

"Why do you say it was my fault, Landry? Was it an insult for me to want to dance with you, and am I the only girl who has no right to enjoy herself as other girls do?"

"It isn't that, Fadette, I have no fault to find with you for wanting to dance with me. I did as you wished, and treated you very well. Your wrongdoing dates farther back than yesterday, and you have not hurt me but yourself, as you ought to know."

"Well, Landry, as true as I love God, I don't know what I have done. I have never given myself a thought, and if I reproach myself for anything, it is that I have, unintentionally, caused you so much annoyance."

"Don't say that Fadette, I have no complaint to make. Let's talk about yourself, and since you don't seem to be conscious of your faults, will you let me tell them to you in all good faith and kindliness?"

"Yes, Landry, I will, and I shall consider it the best reward or the worst punishment you could give me for the good or evil I have done you."

"Well, Fanchon Fadet, since you talk so sensibly, and seem, for the first time in your life, to be gentle and tractable, I will tell you why you are not treated with the respect to which a girl of sixteen is entitled. It is because your appearance and manners are more like a boy's than a girl's. It is because you do not pay any attention to your looks. In the first place, you are not neat and clean, and your language is not what it should be. You know the children have a far worse name for you than Cricket. They often call you a tomboy. Now, do you think it is nice to look more like a boy than a girl when you are sixteen years old? You climb trees like a regular squirrel, and when you jump on a mare, without saddle or bridle, you go off at a gallop, as if the devil were after you. It is all right to be strong and active, and not to be afraid of anything, and it is a natural advantage for a man. But for a woman, there is such a thing as going too far, and you act as if you wanted to attract attention. So people notice you, make fun of you, and shout after you as if you were a wolf. You have a sharp tongue, and you give them answers which are very amusing to those to whom they are not addressed. It is a good thing to be cleverer than other people, but if you show it too plainly, you are sure to make enemies. You are very inquisitive, and when you find out other people's secrets, you cast them in their faces regardless of their feelings, if ever they happen to offend you. This makes them fear you, and people always hate those whom they fear. They give you back worse than they get. And lastly, whether you are a witch or not—and I do think that you know more than you ought about such things, though I hope you have no dealings with the evil one—you try to make people believe that you are one, to frighten those who offend you. All this gives you a bad name. Those are your faults, Fanchon Fadet, and it is because of those faults that nobody likes you. Just think it over and you will see that if you would try and behave a little more like other people, those things in which you excel would be better appreciated."

"Thank you, Landry," answered little Fadette, very gravely, after listening attentively to his lecture. "You have said almost the same things to me which other people tell me, but you have done it kindly and considerately, which is more than the others do. But now, will you listen to what I have to say, and sit down beside me for a few minutes?"

"It is not a very pleasant place," said Landry, who was not

anxious to stay there with her, and who could not help thinking of the evil spells which she was said to cast over those who were not on their guard.

"You think it is not a pleasant place, because you rich people are hard to please. You must have soft grass to sit on out of doors, and you can choose the prettiest and shadiest places in your meadows and gardens. But those who have nothing, do not ask so much of our good Lord and are glad to lay their heads on the first stone they come across. Thorns don't hurt their feet, and everything seems lovely to them in heaven or earth, just wherever they may happen to be. No place is ugly, Landry, to those who know how good everything is which God has made. Without being a witch, I know the use of the least little weed which we tread underfoot; and as I know what they are good for, I examine them, and don't despise either their odour or their looks. Now I tell you this, Landry, so that I may draw your attention to something else, which concerns human creatures' souls, as well as to the garden flowers and roadside weeds. What I mean to say is that we are too apt to despise what seems to us neither good nor beautiful, and by that means we lose a great deal that is useful and salutary."

"I don't understand exactly what you are talking about," said Landry, seating himself beside her, and for a moment they were silent, for Fadette's mind was busy with ideas beyond Landry's comprehension, and as for him, though his head felt rather confused, he could not help listening with pleasure to the girl, for never had he heard a voice so soft, or words so well chosen as Fadette's at that moment.

"Listen, Landry," said she, "I am more to be pitied than

blamed, and if I have injured myself, at least I have never done any serious harm to anybody else, and if people were fair and reasonable in their judgments, they would pay greater heed to my good heart than to my ugly face and my shabby clothes. Just think a minute—or let me tell you if you do not already know—what my life has been ever since I came into the world! I will say nothing against my poor mother, whom everybody blames and abuses, though she is not here to defend herself, and though I can't do it myself, for I don't know just what it was that she did, nor what drove her to it. Well, the world is so wicked that my mother had hardly abandoned me, and I had not yet done crying for her, before the other children, whenever they got the least little bit angry with me—a quarrel over a game, or any trifle, which they would never have noticed in anybody else—would blame me for my mother's sins, and try to make me ashamed of her. Perhaps, in my place, a sensible girl would, as you say, have kept silent, not thinking it prudent to defend her mother, but would have let them abuse her to save herself. But, you see, I couldn't do that. It was of no use to try. My mother was my mother, and whatever she may be, whether I am ever to see her again or not, I shall always love her with all my heart. So when they call me the child of a camp follower or a *vivandière*, I fly into a rage, not on my own account—for I know well enough that it cannot hurt me, as it is not my fault—but for the sake of that poor, dear woman whom it is my duty to defend. And as I do not know how to defend her, I avenge her by telling other people the truths which they deserve to hear, and by showing them that they are no better than the woman at whom they cast a stone. So they call me inquisitive and impertinent because I find out their secrets, and let them be known. The good Lord indeed made me inquisitive, if it is what you call inquisitive to want to know all sorts of hidden things. But if they had treated me decently, I should not have been driven to gratify my curiosity at my neighbours' expense. I should have contented myself with learning those secrets which I get from my grandmother, about curing human ailments, and all about flowers, herbs, stones, insects—all the secrets of nature—there would have been enough of them to occupy and amuse me. I am so fond of roaming about and examining things, I should not have minded being alone, for I should never have been lonely; my greatest pleasure is to haunt unfrequented places and sit there and dream about fifty things which I never hear talked about by people who think themselves very wise and well informed. If I have meddled in my neighbours' affairs, it was only because I wanted to be of service to them, with the little bits of knowledge which I have acquired and by which my grandmother often profits, without saying anything about it. Well, instead of being thanked kindly by all the children of my own age whose wounds and illnesses I had healed, and to whom I had taught my remedies without asking for any reward, I was accused of being a witch, and those who were glad enough to come and ask me for anything when they needed me, afterwards seized the first opportunity to be rude to me.

"This made me furious, and I could easily have had my revenge on them, for if I know beneficial things, I also know many which are injurious. However, I never made any use of them; I don't know what it is to bear malice, and if I revenge myself in words, it is because it is a relief to say just whatever is on the end of my tongue, and then I never give it another thought and for-give and forget as God has commanded. As for not taking care either of my person or my manners, that ought to show you that I am not so silly as to consider myself pretty when I can see that I am so ugly that nobody can bear to look at me. I have heard it often enough to know it, and when I see how harsh and con-temptuous people are to those who have not had their full share of the good gifts of our dear Lord, I take pleasure in shocking them, consoling myself with the thought that my face is not re-pulsive to the good Lord or to my guardian angel, who would no more reproach me for having it than I would reproach them for giving it. I am not one of those who say, There is a caterpillar! Ugly creature! Ah, how hideous it is! Let's kill it!' I would not kill the meanest creature which God has made, and if a caterpil-lar falls into the water, I hold out a leaf for it to crawl upon. For that reason they say that I like all sorts of noxious creatures and that I am a witch because I do not like to hurt a frog, to tear off the legs a wasp, and nail a live bat to a tree. 'Poor thing,' I say, 'if nothing ugly had a right to live, I should have to die as well as you."

XIX

Chapter 19

One way or another Landry was touched when little Fadette spoke so humbly and in such a matter-of-course way of her ugliness, and, recalling her face, of which he could catch only a glimpse on account of the darkness, he said to her, without intending to flatter her, "But, Fadette, you are not so ugly as you think, or as you try to make out. There are a good many uglier people than you, who are never told of it."

"It makes no difference whether I am a little more or a little less ugly—you cannot say, Landry, that I am a pretty girl. Come, don't try to comfort me; for I don't care anything about it."

"Pshaw! Who knows how you would look if you were dressed like the other girls, and had on a pretty cap! One thing everybody acknowledges, that is, if your nose were not so short, your mouth so big, and your skin so dark, you wouldn't be at all bad-looking. They say too, that there is not another such a pair of eyes in all the country round, and if they had not such a bold, defiant expression, anybody would be glad to get a kind glance from them."

Landry said this without much reflection. He found himself recalling all Fadette's good and bad points, and, for the first time, he felt an interest in the subject which he would not have believed possible a short time before. She noticed it, but said nothing about it, being too clever to take it seriously.

"My eyes look kindly on everything good," said she, and with pity on what is not good. Then I don't mind displeasing people who don't please me, and I cannot see how all those pretty girls whom I see admired, can flirt with everybody as if they liked one person as well as another. As for me—if I were pretty—I should not want anyone to think me so, or find me attractive but the one person of whom I was fond."

Landry could not help thinking of Madelon, but little Fadette did not allow him to dwell on that subject. She continued, "So then, Landry, the only wrong I have done other people, is that I have never sought their pity or indulgence for my ugliness. I have shown it to them without any disguise or embellishment, and that offends them and makes them forget that though I have often done them a favour, I have never done them any harm. On the other hand, even if I should take an interest in my appearance, where should I manage to buy finery? Have I ever begged, even though I haven't a cent to bless myself with? What does my grandmother give me beside board and lodging? And if I don't know how to make use of the poor rags my mother left me, is it my fault, since nobody ever took the trouble to teach me, and I have been left to myself since I was ten years old, with nobody to look after me? I know what people say about me, though you are too kind to speak of it. They say that I am sixteen years old and that I could hire myself out, and then I should earn wages enough to support myself. They say that I only stay with my grandmother because I am too lazy and too self-willed to work out, though she does not like me at all, and is well able to keep a servant."

"Well, Fadette, isn't it true?" said Landry. "They say that you are not fond of work, and your grandmother herself says that she would be much better off if she had a servant in your place."

"My grandmother says that because she loves to scold and complain. And yet, whenever I speak of going away, she refuses to let me go, because she knows that I am more useful to her than she will admit. Her eyes and her limbs are not so young as they once were, and she is no longer able to gather the herbs which she uses for her potions and powders, and some of them grow very far off and are difficult to get at. Besides that, as I told you, I know more about some kinds of herbs than she does herself, and she is surprised at the good effects of the medicines I make. As for our animals, they are so fine that everybody is astonished to see such a handsome flock belonging to people who have no pasture of their own. My grandmother knows well enough whom she ought to thank for her good yield of wool, and her rich goat's milk. No, indeed, she doesn't want me to go away, and I am worth a great deal more than I cost her. I am fond of my grandmother, even if she does scold me and give me hardly anything to eat. But I have another reason for staying with her, and I'll tell you, Landry, what it is, if you care to hear."

"Well, go on and tell it," answered Landry, who was greatly interested.

"When I was ten years old my mother left in my care a poor, ugly child—as ugly as I am, and still more unfortunate; for he was born disabled, is sickly, weak, disfigured, and always peevish and ill-tempered because he is always in pain, poor boy! Everybody abuses him, hustles him about, and calls him names, my poor Grasshopper! My grandmother scolds him severely and would beat him too hard if I did not protect him from her by making believe to whip him myself. But I always take care not to hurt him at all, and he knows it well enough. So when he has done anything naughty, he runs and hides under my petticoats, and says, 'Beat me before grandmother gets me!' And I pretend to beat, and the little rascal makes believe to cry. And then I take care of him. I can't always help his being in rags, poor little fellow, but whenever I can manage to get an old garment of any kind, I make it over for him, and I cure him when he is sick, whereas my grandmother would be the death of him, for she doesn't know anything about the care of children. So I look after the poor, sickly little thing, who would suffer if it were not for me, and would soon be in the grave beside my poor father, who died despite all my care. Perhaps I am not doing him a kindness by keeping life in him, misshapen as he is, and so ill-tempered, but I cannot help myself. And when I think of going out to service, Landry, so that I may have some money of my own, and escape from my present wretched condition, my heart aches for him, and I reproach myself as if I were my Grasshopper's mother, and he was about to die through my neglect. So now you know all my faults and shortcomings, Landry. May the dear Lord be my judge! I forgive those who do not understand me."

XX

Chapter 20

Little Fadette's account of herself affected Landry very much, and he could not help acknowledging to himself that her reasoning was unanswerable. At last, he was quite overcome by the way she spoke of her little brother, the Grasshopper, and was seized with a sudden liking for her, which made him feel as if he would be willing to take her part against the whole world.

"Anyone who could blame you, Fadette, is more deserving of blame than you are. You express yourself very well, and nobody would give you credit for having so much good sense and such a kind heart. Why don't you let people see your true self? Then nobody would speak ill of you any more, and there would certainly be some who would do you justice."

"But I told you, Landry," answered she, "that I do not care to please anybody whom I do not like."

"And as you have told me, it must be because—"

Then Landry stopped, taken by surprise by what he found himself about to say. He continued, "Then you must think more of me than you do of anybody else? I always thought you hated me, for I have never been good to you."

"Perhaps I did hate you a little bit," answered little Fadette, "but if I did, I shall never hate you again after today, and I'll tell you why Landry. I thought you were proud, and so you are, but you'll do your duty despite your pride, and you deserve all the more credit. I thought you ungrateful, and though you have been taught to be so proud that it makes you a little ungrateful, you are so true to your word that you keep it whatever it may cost you. And then, I thought you were a coward, and that made me despise you; but I find that you are only superstitious and that you are not wanting in courage when you have real danger to face. You danced with me, though it was a great mortification to you. You even came into church to look for me after Vespers, just as I had forgiven you in my heart after saying my prayers, and had made up my mind not to torment you any more. You protected me from those naughty children, and you defied the big boys who would have ill-treated me if it had not been for you. And then this evening when you heard me crying, you came at once to help and comfort me. Don't imagine, Landry, that I can ever forget such things as that. I will find some means of proving to you, all your life long, that I have not forgotten what you have done for me, and I will always do anything I can for you and at any time. Now, to begin with, I know that I gave you a great deal of trouble today. Yes, Landry, I am sure of it, and I am enough of a witch to have guessed something about you which I did not suspect this morning. Now do believe that I am more mischievous than malicious and that if I had known that you were in love with Madelon, I would not have made trouble between you and her as I did, by making you dance with me. I acknowledge, I thought it was great fun to make you leave a pretty girl to dance with a fright like me, but I supposed that it was only a wound to your vanity. When I came to understand that you were really hurt—that, despite yourself, you could not help looking over at Madelon, and that you were almost ready to cry when you saw how angry she was—I cried myself! Yes, I cried when you wanted to fight her admirers, and you thought they were tears of repentance. That is the reason I was still crying so bitterly when you happened to come upon me here, and I shall never stop crying over it till I have atoned for the trouble I have brought upon such a good boy as I now know you to be."

"Well, my poor Fanchon," said Landry, much moved by the tears which she was beginning to shed afresh, "suppose that you did cause a falling out between me and the girl with whom you think I am in love, what could you do to reconcile us?"

"Leave that to me, Landry," answered little Fadette. "I know enough to explain things satisfactorily. Madelon shall know that it was all my fault. I will tell her everything and will clear you entirely. If she does not make up with you tomorrow, it will be because she has never loved you, and—"

"And then I ought not to feel bad about it, Fanchon. And as she really never has loved me, you would have all your trouble for nothing. So don't do it, and don't worry yourself about the trifling annoyance you have caused me. I have gotten over it already."

Such troubles as that are not so easily healed," answered little

Fadette. Then recollecting herself, she went on, "At least, so they say. You are angry now, Landry. Tomorrow, when you have slept over it, you will feel very unhappy till you have made your peace with pretty Madelon."

"Perhaps I may," said Landry. "But just now, I pledge you my word that I don't understand what you mean, and am not bothering myself about it at all. It seems to me that you are trying to make me believe that I am in love with her, and I really think that if I ever did care for her, it was so little that I can hardly remember it."

"That's strange!" said little Fadette, sighing. "Is that the way you boys love?"

"Pshaw! You girls don't love any better! Just see how little it takes to offend you, and how soon you take up with any new person who happens to come along. But perhaps we are talking about things which we don't understand; at least I don't believe that you know what you are talking about, Fadette; you, who are always making fun of lovers. I've no doubt you think it would be great fun to try and patch up my quarrel with Madelon. Don't do it, I tell you, for she might think that I had asked you to do it, and she would be very much mistaken. Then she might be angry if she thought that I was representing myself as her accepted lover for, to tell the truth, I've never made love to her at all, and even if I did like her society, and was fond of dancing with her, she never encouraged me to say anything to her on the subject. So we had better let the matter drop. She may get over it by herself if she chooses, and if she doesn't, I don't think it will be the death of me."

"I know what you think about that, better than you do yourself, Landry," said little Fadette. "I believe you when you say that you have never told your love to Madelon in so many words, but she must be very stupid if she has not read it in your eyes, especially today. Since I was the cause of your quarrel, I must try and bring you together again, and it would be a good opportunity to let Madelon know that you love her. I will undertake to tell her, and I will do it so delicately and with so much tact, that she can never accuse you of putting it into my head. Just trust your little Fadette, Landry—the poor ugly Cricket whose heart is not so ugly as her face—and forgive my having tormented you; for it will all turn out right. You will find out that if it is pleasant to have a pretty girl in love with you, it is also very convenient to have an ugly girl as a friend; for ugly girls are disinterested and are not so touchy, and don't bear malice for every fancied slight."

"It doesn't make any difference whether you are pretty or ugly, Fanchon," said Landry, taking her hand. "I can see already that your friendship is a very good thing to have—so good, that perhaps it is more to be desired than love. I know now that you must have a good disposition, for I was very rude to you today, and you did not resent it, and though you say that I have treated you well, I know better—I have acted very meanly indeed."

"What do you mean, Landry? I don't know what—"

"Why, I didn't kiss you once in the dance, though it is the custom, and I ought to have done it. I treated you as if you were a little girl of ten, whom no one would take the trouble to kiss, and yet you are almost as old as I am; there isn't more than a year between us. So I really insulted you, and if you were not such a good-hearted girl, you would have noticed it."

"I never once thought of it," said little Fadette, and she got up, for she felt that she was not telling the truth, and she did not want him to find it out. "Come," said she, trying to speak cheerfully, "just hear the crickets chirping in the stubble fields! They are calling me by name, and that owl over there is telling me the hour by the star clock in the sky."

"I hear it too, and I must go back to La Priche, but before I say goodbye Fadette, won't you tell me that you forgive me?"

"But I am not angry with you, Landry, and I have nothing to forgive."

"Yes, you have," said Landry, who felt curiously perturbed since she had been talking to him about love and friendship in so soft a voice that the drowsy chirping of the bullfinches in the thicket seemed harsh in comparison. "Yes, you have something to forgive—and you must let me kiss you now, to make up for not doing it today."

Little Fadette trembled, then recovering her self-possession, she said, "So you want me to let you do penance for your shortcomings. Well, I will acquit you, my boy. It is enough to have danced with the ugly girl, it would be too much to expect you to kiss her, too."

"Ah, don't say that," exclaimed Landry, catching hold of her hand and arm at the same time. "I don't think it would be a penance to kiss you—at least if it didn't offend and annoy you, coming from me—"

And as he said this, he was seized with such a strong desire to kiss little Fadette that he trembled for fear she would not consent.

"Listen, Landry," said she to him in her soft, caressing voice, "if I were a pretty girl, I should tell you that this is neither the place nor the time for kissing, as if we were doing it on the sly. If I were a flirt, I should think, on the contrary, that the time and place were just suitable; for you can't see how ugly I am in the dark, and as there is nobody here, you need not be ashamed of this notion which you have taken into your head. But as I am neither pretty nor a coquette, I must tell you this; just shake hands with me to show that we are friends, and that will be quite enough for me, for I have never had a friend before, and never expect to have another."

"Yes," said Landry, "I'll shake hands with you gladly, but listen, Fadette, the most honest friendship—and that is what I feel for you—need not prevent your allowing me to kiss you. If you will not give me that token of goodwill, I shall think you have something against me."

Then he tried to snatch a kiss, but she resisted, and when he persevered, she began to cry and said, "Let me go, Landry—you hurt my feelings!"

Landry stopped in surprise and was so annoyed to see that she was crying that he was almost angry with her.

"Now I see that you were not telling me the truth when you said that you did not care if nobody else liked you other than me. You like somebody better than you do me, and that is the reason you will not kiss me."

"No, Landry," answered she, sobbing, "but I am afraid that if you kiss me at night when you can't see me, you will hate me when you see me again by daylight."

"Haven't I seen you before?" said Landry, provoked. "Don't I see you this very minute? Just come a little this way, here in the moonlight—I can see you as well as can be, and, pretty or ugly, I like your face, for I like you. That's all I have to say about it."

And then he kissed her—at first quite timidly, and then so increased in his ardour that she grew frightened, and pushed him away, saying, "That will do, Landry. That will do. Anyone would think that you were kissing me because you were angry with me, or that you were thinking of Madelon. Don't worry yourself ! I will speak to her tomorrow, and you will enjoy kissing her a great deal more than you enjoy kissing me."

So she sprang hastily up the bank which led to the road and ran off with her usual light step.

Landry was quite infatuated, and he had a great mind to run after her. He started three times to follow her before he came to the conclusion to go down the river bank. At last, feeling as if the devil was at his heels, he began to run too, and never stopped till he got to La Priche.

The next morning early, as he was feeding his cattle and petting them, he kept thinking of the conversation he had had with little Fadette in the Chaumois road, and which had lasted a full hour, though it seemed to him like a moment. His head was heavy with sleep and the excitement of a day which had turned out contrary to his expectations. He was alarmed and puzzled as he recalled the feeling which had taken possession of him with regard to this girl, whom he now saw in his mind's eye, ugly and ill-dressed as he had always known her. Between whiles, it seemed to him that he must have dreamed of wanting to kiss her, and of pressing her to his heart as if he loved her dearly, and as if she had all of a sudden become the prettiest and dearest girl in the world to him.

"She must be a witch as they say she is, deny it as she may," thought he, "for she certainly bewitched me last night, and never in all my life did I feel such intense love for father, mother, sister, or brother—certainly not for pretty Madelon, and not even for my twin brother Sylvinet—as I felt for that devil of a girl those two or three minutes. If poor Sylvinet could have seen my heart, he would have died of jealousy. My fancy for Madelon did not interfere with my love for my brother but if I should pass a single day of such excitement and infatuation as I felt those few moments when I was with Fadette, I should lose my senses and think there was nobody else in the world."

And Landry felt half dead with shame, fatigue, and vexation. He seated himself on the ox manger, and trembled for fear that the witch had deprived him of his courage, his reason, and his health.

But when it was broad daylight, and the farm labourers of La Priche were all up, they began to tease him about dancing with the ugly Cricket, and they made her out so ugly, so ill-bred, so shabby, that he did not know where to hide his face, he was so ashamed, not only of what they had seen but of what he took good care not to tell them.

But he did not get angry, for the La Priche people were all friendly to him and meant no harm by teasing him. He was even brave enough to tell them that little Fadette was not what they believed her to be—that she was as good as anybody else, and that she was a girl who was capable of doing many a good turn. Then they laughed at him more than ever.

"I won't say anything about her mother," said they, "but as for her—she is a child who doesn't know anything at all, and I advise you not to try any of her remedies on a sick beast, for she is a little chatterbox and she doesn't know anything about curing by magic. But she seems to know how to bewitch boys, for you never left her side all St. Andoche's Day, and you'd better look out, Landry, my boy, or they'll soon call you the Cricket's mate, and the will-o'-the-wisp's double. The devil will get after you. Old Nick himself will come and pull the sheets off our beds and tangle our horses' manes. We shall have to send for the priest to take off the spell she has put upon you."

"I believe," said little Solange, "that he must have put on one of his stockings wrong side out yesterday morning. That attracts witches, and little Fadette must have noticed it."

XXI

Chapter 21

During the day, Landry, who was busy sowing, saw little Fadette pass. She was walking fast and went off in the direction of a coppice where Madelon was cutting leaves for her sheep. It was time to un-yoke the oxen, for they had finished their half day's work, and as Landry was leading them to pasture he watched little Fadette running along with a step so light that the grass hardly bent beneath her tread. He was anxious to know what she was going to tell Madelon, and instead of hurrying off to his dinner, which was waiting for him in the furrow, still warm from the ploughshare he walked on tiptoe along the edge of the wood, to try and hear what the two girls were talking about. He could not see them, and as Madelon muttered her answers, he could not hear what she said, but little Fadette's voice, though soft, was none the less clear, and he did not lose a word, though she spoke in her usual tone. She was talking to Madelon about him, and told her, as she had promised Landry, how, ten months before, she had made him pledge her his word to hold himself at her disposal, whenever she should demand anything of him. And she explained this humbly and so prettily that it was a pleasure to listen to her, and then, without mentioning the will-o'-the-wisp, or how it had frightened Landry, she told about his being almost drowned on the Eve of St. Andoche, by attempting to cross the ford in the wrong place. In short, she represented everything in its best light and made it evident that all the trouble came from a whim of her own, as she wanted to dance with a big boy, instead of the little urchins who had always been her partners.

At this point, Madelon, who was quite out of patience, raised her voice and said, "What is all that to me? You may dance all your life long with the twins of the Twinnery, for all I care. You won't hurt my feelings, I can tell you, and I certainly shall not envy you."

And Fadette answered, "Don't speak so unkindly of poor Landry, for his heart is set on you, and if you don't accept it, you will grieve him more than I can tell you."

She expressed herself so prettily and in so caressing a tone of voice, and lavished such praise on Landry, that he would gladly have borrowed her powers of speech for use on future occasions, and blushed with pleasure to hear himself so eulogized. Madelon was also amazed at little Fadette's pretty manner of speaking, but she despised her too much to let her see how greatly she was impressed.

"You have a nimble tongue, and are as bold as brass," said she, "and it looks as if your grandmother had given you lessons in witchcraft, but I don't like to talk to witches. It's bad luck, and so you will please let me alone, you silly Cricket. You've caught a beau—keep him, my pretty dear, for he is the first and last who will ever take a fancy to your ugly mug. You needn't think I'd take your leavings—no, not if he were a prince. Your Landry is nothing but a fool, and he must be utterly good for nothing, if you, believing that you had taken him away from me, have already come to ask me to take him back. A fine beau for me! A fellow that even little Fadette won't have!"

If that is what is wounding your pride," answered little Fadette, in a tone of voice which went straight to the bottom of Landry's heart, "and if you are so haughty that you will not do him justice till you have first humiliated me, then rest content, Madelon, and trample underfoot the self-respect and spirit of the poor little field Cricket. You say that I must despise Landry or I wouldn't beg you to forgive him. Well, let me tell you, if you care to hear it, that I have been in love with him a long time—that he is the only boy I ever cared for, and that I shall perhaps never care for anybody else as long as I live. But I have too much sense and am also too proud, to fancy that I can ever win his love. He is handsome, rich, and highly esteemed. I am ugly, poor, and despised. I know well enough that he is too good for me, and you must have seen how he scorned me at the festival. So, I say, don't worry, for the man to whom little Fadette would not dare to lift her eyes, loves you dearly. Punish little Fadette by ridiculing her, and by taking possession of him to whom she would not venture to lay claim. If you won't do it out of love for him, you may, at least, do it to punish my insolence—promise me, when he comes to make his peace with you, to treat him kindly, and give him a little encouragement."

Instead of being touched by such humility and self-devotion, Madelon was very scornful indeed, and dismissed little Fadette, saying that she might keep Landry—he would just suit her—but as for herself, he was too childish and too big a fool. But little Fadette's act of self-sacrifice bore fruit despite Madelon's disdain. Such is the perversity of women's hearts, that a boy seems to them a man as soon as he is liked and petted by other women. Madelon, who had never given Landry a serious thought, now began to think about him a great deal as soon as Fadette had gone away. She remembered everything the clever little talker had said to her about Landry's love, and she rejoiced in being able to avenge herself on Fadette, now that she, poor girl, had gone so far as to acknowledge that she was in love with him herself.

That evening she went to La Priche—which was only two or three gunshots away from her own home—and pretending to be in search of one of her own cattle, which had strayed into the same field with her uncle's, she took care that Landry should see her, and encouraged him, with a glance, to come and speak to her.

Landry understood very well, for since he had seen so much of little Fadette his wits had sharpened wonderfully.

"Fadette is a witch," thought he. "She has re-established me in Madelon's good graces, and she has accomplished more for me in a half-hour's chat than I could have done for myself in a year. She is wonderfully clever, and God doesn't often make so good a heart as hers."

And as this thought passed through his mind, he looked at Madelon, but so coldly that she went away before he could make up his mind to go and speak to her. He was not abashed in her presence—strange to say, his shyness had all disappeared, but with it had vanished the pleasure he had once taken in her society, and his desire to win her love.

He had hardly eaten supper when he pretended to be going to bed. He soon got out on the side next to the wall, crept softly out, and started off for the Roulettes ford. This evening, too, the will-o'-the-wisp was flitting about. As soon as he caught sight of it, Landry thought, "So much the better; there is the will-o'-the-wisp. Fadette can't be far off." So he crossed the ford, quite fearlessly, made no misstep, and went up to Mother Fadet's house, keeping a sharp lookout. He waited a little while, but saw no light and heard no noise. Everybody was in bed. He was in hopes that the Cricket, who often prowled about at night after her grandmother and the Grasshopper were asleep, might be wandering somewhere in the neighbourhood. So he set off to try and find her. He crossed the field; he went as far as the Chaumois road, whistling and singing at the top of his voice to attract attention; but he saw nothing but a badger stealing through the stubble, and a screech owl hooting in a treetop. He had to go home without finding an opportunity to thank the girl who had done him such good service.

XXII

⊙⊗⊙

Chapter 22

A whole week passed and Landry did not meet Fadette, which surprised and worried him very much.

"She must still think me ungrateful," said he, "and yet if I haven't succeeded in seeing her, it is not for want of waiting and looking for her. I must have hurt her feelings by kissing her without her consent, yet I meant no harm, and never thought of offending her." And he gave more time to thought this week than he had ever given before in all his life.

His mind was disturbed, he was pensive and agitated, and he could not work without an effort; for neither the big oxen, nor the shining plough, nor the rich red soil, moist with the fine rain of autumn, could fill his thoughts now.

Thursday evening he went to see his twin and found him as anxious as himself. Sylvinet's disposition was unlike his, but they were often in sympathy with each other. He seemed to have divined that something had disturbed his brother's tranquillity, and yet he was far from suspecting what it was. He asked whether he had made up with Madelon, and for the first time in his life, Landry lied to him and said yes. The fact is that Landry had not spoken a word to Madelon, and thought there was plenty of time for that—there was no hurry.

At last, Sunday came, and Landry went to early Mass. He went in before the bell had rung, knowing that little Fadette was in the habit of coming at that time because her prayers were always so long that everybody ridiculed her. He saw a little figure kneeling in the Chapel of the Blessed Virgin—the back turned, and the face hidden in the hands so that there might be nothing to distract the mind. It was little Fadette's posture, but it was not her cap nor dress, and Landry went out again to see if he could not find her on the porch, which we call by a word which signifies the place of rags and tatters, because there are so many ragged beggars there during service. Fadette's rags were the only ones which he did not see. He heard Mass without seeing her, and it was only at the Sursum Corda that, looking once more toward that girl who was praying so fervently in the chapel, he saw her raise her head, and recognized his Cricket, though her whole appearance was totally unfamiliar to him. She still wore the same shabby dress, the coarse woollen petticoat, the red apron, and the linen cap, without the usual lace trimmings; but she had bleached, cutover, and mended everything during the week. She had let down her dress so that it fell over her stockings, at a more suitable length. Her stockings were very white, and so was her cap, which had been altered into the new shape, and sat prettily on her neatly braided black hair. She wore a new neckerchief of a pretty, soft yellow, which suited her dark complexion. She had also lengthened her bodice, and instead of looking like a dressed-up piece of wood, she had a slender, graceful waist like a beautiful honey-bee. Moreover, by washing her face and hands with some unknown tincture of flowers and herbs, her pale face and her dainty little hands looked as fresh and soft as the white blossoms of the spring hawthorn.

Landry, seeing her so changed, let his prayer book drop, and at the noise it made, little Fadette turned quite around and looked at him, and their eyes met. She blushed a little—a pale pink, like the wild hedge rose—but it made her look almost beautiful, especially as her black eyes, which were undeniably lovely, were so brilliant, that she seemed completely transfigured. Landry thought again, "She must be a witch. She has willed to change herself from an ugly girl into a pretty one—and, lo and behold—some miracle has made her beautiful!"

He was really quite awestruck, but that did not prevent his having such a desire to approach and speak to her, that his heart beat with impatience for Mass to be over.

But she did not look at him again, and, instead of scampering about and frolicking with the children after her prayers, she slipped out so quietly that she hardly gave people time to notice the change and improvement in her. Landry did not dare follow her, particularly as Sylvinet never took his eyes off of him; but, about an hour afterwards, he succeeded in getting off, and this time, following the guidance of his heart, he found little Fadette, who was tending her cattle in the little hollow roadway called the Gendarme's Path, because one of the king's gendarmes had been killed there by the people of La Cosse in olden times, as he was trying to compel the poor people to pay the tax and do extra duty, contrary to the requirements of the law, already severe enough.

XXIII

⟨⟩⟨⟩⟨⟩

Chapter 23

As it was Sunday, Fadette was neither sewing nor spinning as she watched her flocks. She was engaged in a simple amusement which our peasant children sometimes take very seriously. She was looking for a four-leaved clover, which is seldom seen, and which brings good luck to those who chance to find it.

"Have you found one, Fanchon," said Landry to her, as soon as he reached her side.

"I have often found them," answered she, " but they don't bring good luck, and I am none the better off for having three sprigs in my book."

Landry sat down beside her as if to have a long talk. But, lo and behold, all of a sudden, he felt more bashful than he had ever felt with Madelon, and though he had a good deal to say, he could not think of a word.

Little Fadette was shy too, for though the twin said nothing, he looked at her with a new expression in his eyes. At last, she asked him why he seemed so surprised at the sight of her.

"Maybe it is because I have made a change in my dress. I have followed your advice, and I thought that if I wanted to appear like a sensible girl, I must begin by dressing myself sensibly. Now I don't dare show myself for fear that people will find fault with me again, and say that I have tried to make myself less ugly, and have not succeeded."

"Let them say what they please," said Landry. "But I don't know what you have done to make yourself pretty; you certainly look lovely today, and nobody with eyes in his head could deny it."

"Don't make fun of me, Landry," answered little Fadette. "They say beauty turns the heads of pretty girls, and ugliness drives ugly girls to desperation. I am used to being a fright, and I should not like to be so foolish as to think that anyone could admire me. But you didn't come to see me about that, and I am waiting to hear that Madelon has forgiven you."

"I didn't come to talk to you about Madelon. I don't know whether she has forgiven me or not, and I haven't asked. I only know that you spoke to her about me, and so kindly that I am very much obliged to you."

"How do you know that I spoke to her about you? She didn't tell you, did she? If she did, you must have made up with her."

"We haven't made up; we don't care enough for each other —she and I—to have a falling out. I know that you spoke to her, for she told somebody who told me."

Little Fadette blushed deeply, which made her look still prettier, for never till today had her cheeks worn that modest glow of timidity and gratification which makes the ugliest face attractive, but at the same time she was anxious lest Madelon had repeated her words, and turned her into ridicule on account of the love which she had confessed for Landry.

"And what did Madelon say about me?" she asked.

"She said that I was a great fool and that none of the girls liked me, not even little Fadette. That little Fadette despised me, ran away from me—had hidden herself a whole week to avoid seeing me, though I had been looking everywhere for her that whole week through. So *I* am a public laughingstock—not *you*, Fadette—because they know that I love you and that you do not return my love."

"What a mean thing to say," answered Fadette, in astonishment, for she was not enough of a witch to guess that Landry was slyer than she. "I would never have believed that Madelon was so untruthful and so deceitful. But we must forgive her, Landry; she says those things out of pique, and she would not be piqued if she did not love you."

"Perhaps that's so," said Landry. "That is why you are not piqued with me, Fanchon. You forgive me everything because you despise everything I do."

"I don't deserve that you should say such things to me, Landry. Now, tell the truth; have I deserved it? I never was so foolish as to tell the lies which they put in my mouth. What I said to Madelon was altogether different. What I told her was for her ear alone, but there was nothing which could injure you—indeed, on the contrary, it should have proved to her how much I thought of you."

"Listen, Fanchon," said Landry, "don't let us dispute as to

what you did or did not say. I want to ask for your advice, you are so clever. Last Sunday, when I met you on the road, I was somehow seized with such an affection for you that I have hardly eaten or slept this whole week. I won't try to hide anything from you, for you are so sharp that it would be of no use. So I will own up that Monday morning I was so ashamed of my love, that I was going to run away, to avoid making such a fool of myself again. But Monday evening it had taken such possession of me once more, that I crossed the ford at night without being at all afraid of the will-o'-the-wisp, though it tried to prevent my looking for you; for it was there again, and when it smiled its wicked smile at me, I smiled back. Every morning since Monday, I feel like a fool, because they tease me about my liking for you, and every evening I feel half crazy because my love for you is stronger than my bashfulness. And now today, you are so pretty and well-mannered that everybody will be as much surprised as I was, and in another fortnight, if you keep on as you have begun, they will not only be ready enough to understand how I could fall in love with you, but there will be a good many in love with you beside myself. Then you will no longer feel under obligation to me for loving you; however, if you have not forgotten last Sunday—St. Andoche's Day—you will remember, too, that I asked you in the Chaumois road to let me kiss you, and that I did it with as much ardour as if you had not been considered ugly and disagreeable. That is all the claim I have to urge, Fadette. Tell me if that will count for anything, or if it makes you angry instead of appealing to your feelings."

Little Fadette's face was buried in her hands, and she did not answer. From what he had heard of her talk with Madelon,

Landry believed that she was in love with him, and I must confess that this conviction of her love for him had aroused in his heart a corresponding affection for her. But when he saw how mortified and downhearted she seemed, he began to fear that she had told Madelon a lie, to bring about the reconciliation which she had undertaken. This worried him, and he fell more in love with her than ever. He drew her hands away from her face and saw that she was as pale as death, and when he bitterly reproached her for not returning his ardent love, she sank to the earth with clasped hands, breathing heavily, for she was suffocating and ready to faint.

XXIV

⁂

Chapter 24

Landry was much alarmed and chafed her hands to restore her to consciousness. They were as cold as ice and as rigid as if made of wood. He rubbed them a long time between his to warm them, and as soon as she could speak, she said to him,

"I think you must be making fun of me, Landry. But there are some subjects too sacred for jesting. Leave me alone, I beg of you, and never speak to me, unless you have a favour to ask of me, in which case I shall always be at your service."

"Fadette, Fadette," said Landry, "you must not say that. It is you who are making fun of me. You hate me, and yet you made me believe the contrary."

"I!" said she, in distress, "what have I ever made you believe? I offered you a sincere affection, such as your twin feels for you, and I have given you perhaps a truer love than his; for I was not jealous, and instead of crossing you in your love affairs, I have done my best to help you."

"That's true," said Landry. "You have behaved like an angel, and I ought to be ashamed to reproach you. Forgive me, Fanchon, and let me love you in my own way. Perhaps it will not be so calm an affection as I have for my twin brother, or my sister Nanette, but I promise not to try and kiss you again if you don't like it." And with a sudden change of sentiment, Landry fancied that little Fadette's affection for him was really a very moderate one, and as he was neither vain nor boastful, he felt as shy and timid in her presence as if he had not heard with his own two ears what she had said about him to Madelon. As for little Fadette, she was clever enough to see, at last, that Landry was head over tail in love with her, and her momentary faintness had been caused by an excess of pleasure at this discovery. But she was afraid that happiness so quickly won might be very short-lived. It was this fear which led her to wish to give Landry time to conceive a strong desire for her love. He stayed with her till dark, for, though he no longer dared make love to her, he took such pleasure in looking at her and hearing her speak that he could not bear to leave her a moment. He played with the Grasshopper, who was never far away from his sister, and who soon came and joined them. He was good to him and soon saw that the poor little thing, whom everybody ill-treated, was neither silly nor naughty with those who were kind to him. Indeed, at the end of an hour, he was so far civilized and so grateful, that he kissed the twin's hands, and called him dear Landry just as he called his sister dear Fanchon. Landry was touched and pitied him, and it seemed to him that he and everybody else had neglected their duty toward these poor children of Mother Fadet's, who only needed a little of the love which other youngsters get, to become better than any of them. The few succeeding days Landry managed to see little Fadette, sometimes in the evening, when he had a chance to have a little chat with her, and sometimes in the daytime, when he happened to meet her in the fields; and though she was not able to stop long, as she would not and could not neglect her work, he was glad of the opportunity to say a few words to her, straight from his heart, and to devour her with his eyes. And she continued to dress neatly and to talk and behave nicely to everybody so that it attracted notice, and it was not long before people began to treat her very differently. As she no longer did anything out of the way, she was no longer insulted, and when she saw that, she no longer felt any temptation to use bad language or annoy anybody. But as public opinion is slower to change than our individual resolutions, some time was required to transform into esteem and approval the contempt and dislike which had been the general feeling toward her. You shall hear later how this change came about. But for the present, you may imagine that nobody placed much confidence in little Fadette's reformation. Four or five of those good old men and women, who are lenient in their judgment of young people growing up around them, and who act the part of fathers and mothers to the whole neighbourhood, sometimes met to have a chat under the walnut trees of La Cosse, and watch the youngsters swarming around them, dancing and playing quoits. And these old people would say, "So-and-so will make a fine soldier if he keeps on, for he is too well built to be exempted from service; that boy will be clever and sharp like his father; that one over there will be as intelligent and even-tempered as his mother; that young Lucette will certainly make a good farm servant. Big Louise will have plenty of admirers, and as for little Marion, she'll have as much sense as the others by the time she is grown up."

And when it came little Fadette's turn to be criticised and have judgment passed on her, they said, "Look at her hurry past, without stopping to sing or dance. We haven't seen anything of her since St. Andoche's Day. It must be that she was dreadfully shocked when the children from hereabouts pulled off her cap in the dance, so she has altered her helmet and now she looks as well as anybody."

"Have you noticed how much fairer her skin has grown lately?" said Mother Couturier, one day. "Her face used to be so covered with freckles that it looked like a quail's egg, and the last time I saw her close up I was astonished to see how white she was. She even looked so pale that I asked her if she had had the fever. Judging from present appearances, it really looks as if she might continue to improve, and—who can tell—many an ugly girl turns out to be pretty by the time she is seventeen or eighteen years old."

"And then they come to have some sense," said Father Naubin, "and a girl learns to make herself attractive and agreeable. It is high time for the Cricket to realize that she is not a boy. Good heavens! We all thought she'd turn out a perfect disgrace to the place. But she'll settle down and come out all right like the others. She will feel that she must behave herself so that people will forget that she had such a good-for-nothing mother, and you'll see, she won't get herself talked about."

"God grant that she may," said Mother Courtillet, "for it is a pity to see a girl look like a runaway horse. But I have some hopes of Fadette, for I met her yesterday, and instead of hobbling along behind me as usual, imitating my limp, she said good morning and asked after my health as nicely as anybody."

"That little girl you are all talking about is more wild than bad," said Father Henri. "She has a good heart, I can tell you, for she has often taken my grandchildren out to the fields with her, just to relieve my daughter, when she was ill, and she took such good care of them that they wanted to stay with her."

"They tell me," said Father Couturier, "that one of Father Barbeau's twins fell in love with her on St. Andoche's Day. Is it true?"

"Nonsense!" answered Father Naubin. "You mustn't place any faith in that story. It was only a childish fancy, and the Barbeaus are no fools—children or parents—let me tell you."

And so, they talked about little Fadette, but nobody thought of her very often, for they hardly ever saw her.

XXV

Chapter 25

But there was one person who saw her very often and was greatly interested in her, and that was Landry Barbeau. He was beside himself when he could not manage to get a few words with her, but as soon as he was in her presence a moment, he was soothed and contented, for she talked sensibly to him, and sympathized with his feelings. Perhaps her treatment of him was not altogether free from coquetry—at least, so it seemed to him—but as her motive was honourable, and she would not allow him to make love to her, till she had duly considered the matter, he had no right to complain. She could not suspect him of trying to deceive her as to the ardour of his affection for her, for it was such love as is not often found among country people, who are less impulsive and passionate than the dwellers in cities. Indeed Landry was by nature rather more than usually phlegmatic, and nobody could have foreseen that he would singe his wings so severely. His secret was carefully hidden, and it would have been a great surprise to anyone who had discovered it. But Fadette, seeing that he had given his heart to her so suddenly and unreservedly, was afraid that it might be only a flash in the pan, or that her own feelings might become more interested than was seemly for two children, not yet of marriageable age, at least according to the judgment of their parents and the dictates of prudence; for love is impatient of delay, and when it is once kindled in the hearts of two youngsters, it is a miracle, indeed, if it waits for the approval of others.

But little Fadette, who had always seemed younger than she really was, had plenty of sense, and a power of will far in advance of her age. She must have had extraordinary strength of mind to produce this result, for hers was a passionate nature—more so, indeed, than Landry's. She was desperately in love with him, and yet she behaved with remarkable discretion, for though she thought of him constantly, day and night, and longed to see him and caress him, she controlled herself as soon as she saw him, talked calmly and sensibly to him, even pretending that she did not know what it was to love passionately, and allowing him simply to shake hands with her.

And Landry, who was so greatly infatuated with her that, when he was alone with her in secluded places or under cover of the darkness, he might so far have forgotten himself as to refuse to obey her, was nevertheless so afraid of her displeasure, and so uncertain that she really loved him, that he was on as innocent terms with her as if she had been his sister, and he Jeanet, the little Grasshopper.

Fadette, to turn his attention from ideas which she did not

wish to encourage, tried to teach him all the things she knew, and her intelligence and natural ability had carried her far beyond her grandmother's instructions. She did not try to keep up any appearance of mystery with Landry, and as he had always had a fear of witchcraft, she tried her best to make him understand that the devil had nothing to do with the secrets of her science.

"Pshaw, Landry," she said to him one day, "there is no such thing as the intervention of the evil spirit. There is only one spirit, and that is a good one, for it is the spirit of God. Lucifer is an invention of the Curé's, and Old Nick is an old wife's tale. When I was a little thing, I believed in all those stories and stood in great awe of my grandmother's evil spells, but she laughed me out of it; for, to tell the truth, those who doubt everything are the ones who try to impose on others, and nobody has less faith in the devil than the witches themselves, though they are always invoking him on all occasions. They know well enough that they have never seen him or received the slightest aid from him. Those who are so silly as to believe in him and try to call him up, have never succeeded in getting him to appear. For instance, there was the miller of Passe-aux-chiens, who, as my grandmother told me, used to go to a place where four roads meet, carrying a big cudgel, and there he would summon the devil, intending to give him a sound thrashing. And they heard him shouting in the night, 'Are you coming, you devil?

Are you coming, mad dog? Are you coming, Old Nick?' But no Old Nick ever made an appearance. So the miller was quite eaten up with vanity, for he thought the devil was afraid of him."

"But, my little Fanchon," said Landry, "it isn't exactly Christian not to believe in the devil."

"I can't argue about it," said she, "but if he does exist, I am quite sure that he has no power to come on earth and do us any harm or steal away our souls from God. He could never have the insolence to do that, and since the earth is the Lord's, He alone can govern the men and things which dwell on it."

So Landry laid aside his foolish fears, and could not help wondering to see little Fadette so good a Christian in all her ways of thinking, and in her prayers. Indeed her piety took a more attractive form than that of other people. She loved God with all the fervour of her nature, for her keen intelligence and her tender heart were apparent in everything she did. When she spoke to Landry of this love, he was amazed to discover that he had been taught to repeat certain prayers and practise certain observances without the remotest idea of their meaning and that though he had always treated sacred things with reverence from a sense of duty, his heart had never glowed with love for his Creator as little Fadette's did.

XXVI

Chapter 26

In his walks and talks with her, he became acquainted with the properties of herbs and with all sorts of recipes for curing man and beast. He soon tried the effect of one of the latter on one of Father Caillaud's cows, which had eaten too much green food, and was swollen up with the colic. As the veterinarian had given her up, saying that she could not live an hour, Landry gave her a potion which little Fadette had taught him to prepare. He told nobody what he had done, and the next morning when the workmen—very sorry for the loss of so fine a cow—came to bury her, they found her standing up, beginning to sniff at her food; her eyes were bright and the swelling had almost entirely disappeared. Another time, a colt was bitten by a viper, and Landry, still following the directions of little Fadette, cured it in short order. Finally, he had an opportunity of trying the antidote for rabies on one of the La Priche dogs, who got well before he had bitten anybody. As Landry did his best to hide his intimacy with little Fadette, he did not boast of his skill, and the cure of his cattle was attributed to the care which he took of them. But Father Caillaud, who had a good knowledge of veterinary practice, like all good farmers, was surprised and said, "Father Barbeau has no special talent for cattle raising, and hasn't even very good luck at it, for he lost several fine cattle last year, and not for the first time. But Landry has the knack of it, and that is something one is born with. You have it or you don't have it, and even if one should go and study in the schools as the veterinary surgeons do, it is no use unless it is born in you. Now, I tell you, Landry is clever, and so he finds out what remedies to use. It is a great gift which nature has bestowed on him, and it will be worth more than capital to him in the management of a farm."

Father Caillaud's opinion was not that of a credulous or ignorant man, only he was mistaken when he took it for granted that Landry's skill was a gift of nature. Landry had no gift, save carefulness and intelligence in the use of the prescriptions which had been taught him. Still, there is such a thing as a natural gift, for little Fadette had it, and with the few simple lessons which she had received from her grandmother, she recognized the salutary properties which God has bestowed on certain plants, which are to be employed in special ways, and showed as much readiness as if she had discovered them herself. She told the truth when she declared that she never resorted to witchcraft, but she was very observing, and made experiments, drew inferences, noticed, and made comparisons, and nobody can deny that this is a natural gift. Father Caillaud went still further—he believed that there are some herdsmen and labourers who are more or less lucky than others and that the very presence of such people in the stable benefits or injures the animals. However, as there is always a little truth in the greatest delusions, it must be acknowledged that good care, cleanliness, and conscientious labour will succeed, where negligence or stupidity will cause disaster.

Landry's tastes had always run in that direction. His love for Fadette was increased by the gratitude which he felt for the information which she had given him, and the respect which her talents and cleverness inspired. He was thankful enough to her now for frowning down his lovemaking in their walks and talks, and he saw, too, that she had her lover's interests and improvement more at heart than the pleasure she might have experienced if she had allowed him to court and flatter her as he had at first wished to do. Landry was soon so much in love that he was no longer ashamed to have it known that he had given his heart to a girl who had the reputation of being ugly, ill-tempered, and badly brought up. If he still observed any precautions, it was on account of his twin brother, whose jealous disposition was well known to him, and who had been obliged to make a great effort to resign himself to Landry's fancy for Madelon—a very mild and tame affair in comparison with what he now felt for Fanchon Fadet.

But if Landry was too eager in his love to think of prudence, little Fadette, on the other hand, had a natural fondness for mystery. Besides that, she did not want to expose him to being teased about her. Little Fadette, in short, loved him too well to wish to make trouble between him and his family and enjoined upon him such secrecy that it was almost a year before anybody suspected that there was anything between them. Landry had cured

Sylvinet of prying into his affairs, and that part of the country, which is sparsely inhabited and thickly wooded, affords many facilities for lovers to meet in secret. Sylvinet, seeing that Landry no longer gave a thought to Madelon, though he had brought himself to regard sharing his brother's affection with her as a necessary evil, made more endurable by Landry's bashfulness and the girl's prudence, was rejoiced to find that Landry was in no hurry to withdraw his affection from his brother, to bestow it on a woman, and, being no longer jealous, he left him with more freedom to do what he liked and go where he pleased on fete days and holy days. Landry found plenty of pretexts for coming and going, especially on Sunday evenings, when he left the Twinnery early and did not go home to La Priche till almost midnight. He had no difficulty in getting in, for he had persuaded them to let him have a little bed in the Capharnion.[1] You will perhaps take me up on this word, for the schoolmaster objects to it and insists on calling it Capharnaum, but however much he may know about the word, he knows nothing about the thing, for I had to explain to him that it was that part of a barn, near the stables, where they keep the yokes, chains, horseshoes, and all sorts of utensils used for the farm animals, and for the cultivation of the land. So Landry could go home at any hour he pleased without waking anybody, and he always had all day Sunday to himself and till Monday morning, because Father Caillaud and his eldest son, who were both very steady men and never frequented wine shops or drank to excess on holidays, were in the habit of assuming all the care and management of the farm on such occasions, in order, said they, that all the young people of the establishment, who worked harder than they did during the week, might be free to frolic and amuse themselves, as our good Lord intended them to do.

And in the wintertime, when the nights are so cold that love-making would have been very uncomfortable in the open air, Landry and little Fadette found a safe shelter in the Jacot Tower, an old deserted dovecote, which the pigeons had abandoned years ago, but which was still sound and weathertight. It was attached to Father Caillaud's farm, and he still used it for storing his surplus crops. As Landry kept the key and the dovecote stood on the border of the La Priche property, not far from the Roulettes ford, and in the middle of a walled field of alfalfa, it would have puzzled the devil himself to discover the rendezvous of this pair of young lovers. When the weather was mild, they wandered about the groves of young trees, fit for cutting, which are numerous in this part of the country. They form admirable hiding places for thieves and lovers, and as we have no thieves among us, only the lovers avail themselves of their shelter and find themselves undisturbed and free from annoyance.

NOTES

1. Capharnion. This word with its correct spelling, Capharnaum, is much used in France. Capharnaum or Capernaum was a large commercial town in Judea, hence its vulgar meaning, a place where many things are stored. Littré, *Dict. de la langue française*.

XXVII

~⧖~

Chapter 27

But as secrecy cannot be maintained forever, it happened that, as Sylvinet was passing along by the cemetery wall one fine Sunday, he heard the voice of his twin a few steps away from him. Landry's tones were low, but Sylvinet was so well acquainted with his voice that he could have guessed what he was talking about, even if he had not heard a single word.

"Why won't you come and dance?" said he to a person whom Sylvinet could not see. "It is so long since you have been seen to stay after Mass, that nobody will think anything of it if I dance with you, as I am supposed to be only slightly acquainted with you. They will not think that I do it for love of you, but for politeness' sake, and because I want to see whether you have forgotten how to dance."

"No, Landry, no," answered a voice which Sylvinet did not recognize, because it was so long since he had heard it, little

Fadette having kept herself so aloof from everybody, and particularly from him.

"No," said she, "it is better that I should not attract attention, and if you danced with me once, you would want to do it every Sunday, and that would be more than enough to make people talk about us. Believe what I have always told you, Landry—the day when our love is discovered, our troubles will begin. Let me go, and after you have spent a part of the day with your family and your twin brother, you may come and meet me at the place which we agreed upon."

"But it is so melancholy never to dance," said Landry. "You used to be so fond of dancing, darling, and you danced so well! How delighted I should be to take you by the hand, and whirl you about in my arms, and to see you dance with nobody but me—you who are so graceful and light-footed!"

"That is just what I must not do," answered she. "But I see that you are longing to dance, my dear Landry, and there is no reason why you should give it up. Go and dance a little! I shall be glad to know that you are enjoying yourself, and I shall wait for you as patiently as possible."

"Oh, you have too much patience!" said Landry, in a voice which was indicative of a very slender supply of that virtue, "but I would rather have my legs cut off than dance with girls I do not like, and whom I wouldn't kiss for a hundred francs."

"Well, if I should dance," answered little Fadette, "I could not help dancing with other young men beside you, and I should have to let them kiss me too."

"Go home then, go home, as quick as you can!" said Landry. "I don't want anybody to kiss you." Sylvinet heard nothing further except the sound of retreating footsteps, and he slipped quickly into the cemetery and let his brother pass, for he did not want to be caught eavesdropping by him.

This discovery was like a stab in the heart to Sylvinet. He did not try to find out what girl it was with whom Landry was so desperately in love. It was enough for him to know that there was a person for whose sake Landry was willing to give him up, to whom he devoted all his thought so that he no longer told his twin brother everything which concerned him.

"He must have lost confidence in me," thought he, "and this girl of whom he is so fond must put it into his head to fear and dislike me. I am not surprised now, that he is always so bored at home, and so restless when I go out to walk with him. I gave it up, thinking that he would rather be alone, but now I shall be very careful not to annoy him. I shall not say anything to him, for he would be angry with me for finding out what he did not want me to know. I shall be the only sufferer and he will be glad to get rid of me."

Sylvinet kept his resolution, and even went farther than necessary, for not only did he give up all attempts to keep his brother with him, but, to leave him free to do just as he chose, he was always the first to leave the house, and went wandering about the orchard, never going out into the field, saying to himself, "If I should happen to meet Landry, he might think that I was watching him, and would let me know that he thought me a nuisance."

And so it came to pass that, by degrees, his old trouble, which had been almost cured, took such firm and obstinate hold on him, that it soon betrayed itself in his face. His mother reproved him gently, but, as he was ashamed to own that he was as child-ish at eighteen as he had been three years earlier, he would not confess what was troubling him.

This saved him from an illness, for our good Lord never deserts those who try to help themselves, and he who dares to keep his troubles to himself is more able to bear them than he who utters a complaint. The poor twin began to look pale and sad all the time; he had an occasional attack of fever, and as he was not done growing he continued to be quite slender and deli-cate. He could not work very steadily, but that was not his fault, for he knew that work was good for him. It was bad enough to worry his father by his melancholy—he did not want to irri-tate and wrong him by his listlessness. So he went to work and worked all the harder because he was out of patience with him-self. So he often exceeded his strength and was so tired the next day that he could not do anything.

"He will never make a stout worker," said Father Barbeau, "but he does the best he can, and does not spare himself even when he might do so. That is the reason why I do not want to hire him out, for between his dread of a scolding, and the small amount of strength which God has given him, he would be sure to kill himself, and I should reproach myself for it the rest of my life."

Mother Barbeau took the same view of the matter which he did and tried her best to cheer up Sylvinet. She consulted sev-eral doctors regarding his health, and some of them told her to take great care of him and let him drink nothing but milk be-cause he was delicate, while others said to keep him at work and give him good wine, because, being delicate, he needed strengthening. Mother Barbeau did not know which to believe, which is always the case when one has too many advisers.

As she could not come to a decision, she, fortunately, did nothing, and Sylvinet kept on in the way which the good Lord had laid out for him, without meeting anything to turn him either to the right or to the left, and he bore his little cross and did not break down utterly under his trial, up to the time when Landry's love affair was made public, and Sylvinet's distress was increased by the sight of his brother's suffering.

XXVIII

Chapter 28

Madelon was the first to discover the secret, and she made a bad use of her knowledge, which she had happened upon quite by accident. She had long ago consoled herself for Landry's desertion, and as she had not wasted much time loving him, it did not take her long to forget him. However, she still bore him a little grudge, which only needed an opportunity to show itself—so true it is that a woman's pique outlives her liking.

This is the way the thing came about. Pretty Madelon, who was celebrated for her discretion and high and mighty airs with boys, was at heart a genuine coquette, and not half so faithful and sincere in her attachments as the poor Cricket, of whom everybody spoke and prophesied ill. Madelon had already had two admirers, not counting Landry, and now had her eye on a third—her cousin, the youngest son of Father Caillaud de La Priche. She had taken so great a fancy to him that she consented to accompany him to the dovecote which Landry and little Fadette had used as a trysting place for their innocent love-making. She did not know of any other place where she could have a private interview with her new sweetheart and feared an outburst from the last man she had encouraged, for she was aware that he was watching her.

Young Caillaud had made a great search for the key of the dovecote, but without success, as it was still in Landry's pocket; he had not dared ask anybody for it, because he had no good reasons to give in explanation. Nobody but Landry cared anything about the whereabouts of the key, and so young Caillaud, taking it for granted that it must be lost, or that his father had it on his bunch, determined to break in the door. But the day this happened, Landry and Fadette were already there, and the two pairs of lovers felt so silly when they found themselves face to face, that they were all equally anxious to keep the secret. But Madelon was so angry and jealous when she saw that Landry—who was now one of the best-looking and most promising young fellows in the neighbourhood—had remained faithful to little Fadette ever since St. Andoche's Day, that she resolved to have her revenge. She said nothing about it to young Caillaud, who was an honest man and would not have given her any assistance, but she took into her confidence one or two young girls of her acquaintance, who were also rather miffed because Landry never asked them to dance anymore, and they kept such close watch on little Fadette that it was not long before they found out all about her intimacy with Landry.

After seeing them together two or three times, they noised it abroad throughout the neighbourhood, telling everybody who would listen to them—and heaven knows there are always plenty of tongues to spread scandal and ears to hearken to it—that Landry was on very familiar terms with little Fadette.

Then all the girls took it up, for when a good-looking youngster with property devotes himself to a young woman, the others regard it as an insult to their charms, and they will miss no opportunity of saying something disagreeable about her. We may add, too, that when women undertake to spread a piece of gossip, it flies like wildfire.

So, two weeks after the adventure in Jacot's Tower, everybody, little and big, old and young, knew that Landry the twin was in love with Fanchon the Cricket. There was no mention made of the tower, however, or of Madelon, who took good care to keep in the background, and even pretended to be surprised at a piece of news which she had been the first to set in circulation.

The rumour reached the ears of Mother Barbeau, who was much distressed and hesitated to speak to her husband on the subject. But Father Barbeau heard it from somebody else, and Sylvinet, who had carefully kept his brother's secret, was worried to find out that everybody knew it.

So one evening when Landry was about to leave the Twinnery rather early, as he was in the habit of doing, his father said to him, in the presence of his mother, his elder sister, and his twin brother, "Don't be in such a hurry to leave us, Landry—I have something to say to you. I'll wait till your godfather comes, for I want to ask you for an explanation before all those members of the family who are interested in your welfare."

When Landry's godfather, Uncle Landriche, had arrived, Father Barbeau began. "What I am about to say will be rather mortifying to you, Landry; indeed I am myself both sorry and ashamed to be forced to question you before the whole family. But I am in hopes that this mortification will do you good, and cure you of a fancy which might injure you very much. It seems that you have made an acquaintance dating back to last St. Andoche's Day—nearly a year ago. I was told of it at the time, for it was most extraordinary that you should dance all day with the ugliest, dirtiest, and most disreputable girl in all our part of the country. I thought best to take no notice of it, thinking that you had merely done it by way of amusement; I did not approve of such behaviour, for if it is wrong to associate with bad people, you should never do anything to increase their degradation, and expose them to the contempt of everybody. I neglected saying anything to you about it, thinking, when I saw how low-spirited you looked the next day, that you were sorry for what you had done, and would not be likely to do it again. But now, this last week, I hear quite a different story, and although the report comes from reliable people, I shall not believe it unless you acknowledge its truth. If I have wronged you by my suspicions, you must attribute it to my interest in you, and to the fact that I consider it my duty to keep an eye on you. If the story is false, I shall be glad to take your word for it, and it will be a relief to know that you have been slandered."

"Father," said Landry, "will you be good enough to tell me of what you accuse me? I will answer you truthfully and with all due respect."

"I think I have already told you enough to make you understand, Landry, that you are accused of improper relations with the granddaughter of Mother Fadet, who is bad enough, not to speak of the unfortunate girl's own mother, who ran away from her husband, her children, and her native place, to be a camp follower. They say that you wander about everywhere with little Fadette, which makes me fear that she has inveigled you into some disreputable love affair, which you may regret all your life long. Now, do you understand?"

"I understand perfectly, my dear father," answered Landry, "but allow me to ask you one question before I answer you. Is it on account of her family or only on her own account, that you regard Fanchon Fadet as an undesirable acquaintance for me to have?"

"For both reasons, of course," answered Father Barbeau, with rather more severity than he had shown at the beginning of the conversation, for he had expected to find Landry very humble and penitent, whereas he was perfectly calm and prepared for anything. "In the first place," said he, "she comes of very disreputable stock, and no decent, respectable family like mine would be willing to connect itself with the Fadets. In the next place, nobody has any confidence in little Fadette herself or any respect for her. We have seen her grow up and we know all about her. They tell me—and indeed I have noticed it myself two or three times—that for the past year she has behaved herself better; that she has stopped running around with the little boys, and is no longer impudent to everybody she meets. You see that I want to be perfectly just, but that does not prevent my seeing that a child who has had such a bringing up can never make a decent woman, and knowing her grandmother as I do, I have every reason to believe that the whole affair is a put-up job to entrap you into making promises which will place you in a very mortifying and embarrassing position. People even go so far as to say that the girl is in a delicate situation. I am not willing to believe this on mere hearsay, but if it should turn out to be true, you would surely be suspected and it might result in a scandal and a lawsuit."

Landry, who from the first word had made up his mind to be on his guard and keep his temper, now lost all patience. He turned as red as fire, and said, rising from his seat, "Father, the people who told you that lied like dogs. It is such an outrageous insult to Fanchon Fadet, that if I had them here, I should have made them take back their words, or fight it out with me. Tell them that they are cowards and heathens—just let them say to my face what they have been mean enough to insinuate to you behind my back, and we'll see how it will turn out."

"Don't fly into such a rage, Landry," said Sylvinet, in the greatest distress. "Father does not mean to accuse you of ruining the girl, but he is afraid that she may have been imprudent with others, and now wants to make it appear, by hanging around you all the time, that she has some claim on you."

XXIX

Chapter 29

His twin brother's voice had a soothing effect on Landry, but he could not allow his words to pass without a reply.

"Brother," said he, "you don't know anything at all about it. You have always been prejudiced against little Fadette, and you don't know her at all. I care very little for what they say against me, but I will not allow them to talk against her, and I want my father and mother to know that there isn't another girl in the world so modest, so sensible, so good, and so unselfish as she is. If she is so unfortunate as to have disreputable relatives, she deserves all the more credit for being what she is, and I would never have believed it possible that Christian people could blame her for her unfortunate birth."

"You seem to think that I am to blame, Landry," said Father Barbeau, rising too, to show that he did not wish any more words on the subject. "It is very plain to be seen that you are more interested in this Fadette than I could have wished. Since you are neither sorry nor ashamed of what you have done, we will say no more about it. I shall think over what I had better do, to save you from the consequences of a piece of youthful folly. And now you had better return to your employer."

"You must not go off like that," said Sylvinet, detaining his brother, who was about to leave. "Father, Landry is so sorry for having offended you that he cannot say anything. Forgive him and kiss him, or he will cry all night long, and your displeasure will be a greater punishment than he deserves."

Sylvinet was crying, Mother Barbeau was crying, too, and so were the elder sister and Uncle Landriche. Nobody's eyes were dry but Father Barbeau's and Landry's, but their hearts were full, and they kissed each other as the rest of the family begged them to do. The father did not exact any promise from his son, knowing that such promises are very uncertain in an affair of this kind, and not wishing to run any risk of being disobeyed, but he gave Landry to understand that the matter did not drop there and that he should take it up again.

Landry went away, indignant and distressed. Sylvinet would have been glad to follow him, but he did not dare do so, for he took it for granted that his brother would go straight to little Fadette to tell her of his troubles, and he went to bed so downhearted that he did nothing but sigh all night and dream that some dreadful misfortune had overtaken the family.

Landry went to little Fadette's and knocked at the door. Mother Fadet had grown so deaf that nothing could waken her, after she had once fallen asleep, and ever since Landry had found out that his secret was discovered, he could not get a chance to talk to Fanchon, excepting at night, in the room where the old woman and little Jeanet were sleeping. Even then he ran a great risk, for the old witch could not bear him, and would have greeted him with more cuffs than pretty speeches. Landry told all his troubles to little Fadette and found her perfectly resigned and fearless. At first, she tried to persuade him that it would be better for him to think no more about her. But when she saw that he grew more and more indignant and distressed, she urged him to submit, telling him that everything would turn out all right.

"Listen, Landry," said she, "I have always foreseen what has just happened, and I have often wondered what we should do in such a case as the present. Your father is right and I do not blame him at all, for it is his affection for you which makes him dread to see you fall in love with a girl like me. I forgive him for his pride and for being rather unjust to me, for we can't deny that I was as wild as a hawk when I was little, and you yourself gave me a good talking to the day you fell in love with me. Even if I have cured myself of some of my faults the past year, there has not been time enough to inspire your father with confidence in me, as he told you today. We must wait a while longer, and by degrees, the prejudice against me will die out, and the wicked lies they are telling will be forgotten. Your father and mother will see that I am a decent girl and that I am not trying to corrupt you or get money out of you. They will do justice to the sincerity of my affection for you, and we shall be able to see and talk to each other, and nobody will object. But meanwhile, we must obey your father, who will forbid you visiting me, I am sure."

"I shall never have the courage to give up seeing you," said Landry. "I would rather go and throw myself into the river."

"Then I must have it for you," said Fadette. "I will go away, I will leave this part of the country for a little while. There is a good place in the city which has been waiting for me for the last two months. My grandmother is getting so old and so deaf that she has almost given up making and selling her medicines, and cannot hold consultations any more. She has a relative—a very good woman—who has offered to come and live with her, and who will take good care of her and my little Grasshopper—"

Little Fadette's voice broke down a moment at the thought of leaving this child, whom, next to Landry, she loved better than anything in the world, but she mustered up the courage to go on. "He is strong enough now to get along without me. He is going to make his first communion, and he will take so much interest in going to catechism with the other children, that he will forget to grieve about my going away. You must have noticed how sensible he is getting to be, and that the other boys do not tease him as much as they used to do. Now, Landry, you must see that there is no other way. People must have time to forget me a little, for just now there is a good deal of ill-feeling against me in the neighbourhood. When I come back again after being away for a year or two and bring good references and an unblemished reputation, which I can gain elsewhere more easily than I could here, they will stop tormenting us, and we shall be better friends than ever."

Landry would not listen to this plan; he was quite overcome with grief and went back to La Priche in a state of mind which would have moved the hardest heart to pity.

Two days afterwards, as he was taking the tub to the vintage, young Caillaud said to him, "I see you are angry with me, Landry, and it is some time since you have spoken to me. You probably think that I spread abroad the report of your love affair with little Fadette, and I am sorry that you could think me capable of such a piece of meanness. As true as there is a God in heaven, I have never breathed a single word on the subject, and I am really troubled that you should have had so much to worry you, for I always thought a good deal of you, and I never bothered little Fadette. I'll even say that I respect the girl for what happened at the dovecote, for she might have gossiped if she had chosen, and yet she has held her tongue so that nobody knows anything about it. She might have made use of what she knew if only to revenge her-self on Madelon, for she must know well enough who has started all these stories. But she hasn't done it, and I see, Landry, that it isn't safe to judge people by appearances or reputation. Fadette, who had the name of being a bad girl, has turned out to be very kind-hearted. Madelon, who was considered good, has acted very deceitfully, not only toward Fadette and you but toward me, too, for she has given me good reason to doubt her fidelity to me."

Landry took young Caillaud's explanation in good part, and the latter did his best to comfort him in his trouble.

"You have been very badly treated, my poor Landry," said he, in conclusion, "but little Fadette's good behaviour ought to be a great source of consolation to you. It is good of her to go away to put an end to the trouble in your family, and I have just told her so, as I said goodbye to her when she went by."

"What are you talking about, Caillaud? " exclaimed Landry. "Is she going away? Has she gone?"

"Didn't you know it?" said Caillaud. "I supposed that you had settled it between you and that you did not accompany her for fear of making people talk. But she's going away, that you may depend on. She passed right by our house, not more than a quarter of an hour ago, and she had her little bundle under her arm. She was going to Château Meillant, and she cannot be farther off by this time than Vielle Ville or Ormont Hill."

Landry left his goad resting against the straw pad of his oxen—started off and never stopped till he caught up with little Fadette, in the sandy road which leads down from the Ormont vineyard to Frenelaine.

Then, exhausted by grief and the haste with which he had come, he fell down across the pathway, unable to speak a word, but making signs to her that she must walk over his prostrate body if she wished to get rid of him. When he had somewhat recovered, Fadette said to him, "I wanted to save you this grief, Landry, and now you are doing all you can to unnerve me. Be a man, and do not break down my spirit! I have more need of courage than you imagine, and when I think of little Jeanet looking for me and crying after me at this very moment, my strength fails me so that I am ready to dash my head against these stones. Ah, I beg of you, Landry, help me, instead of trying to make me forget my duty, for if I don't go away today, I shall never go, and we shall be ruined."

"Fanchon, Fanchon! You have no such great need of courage!" answered Landry. "You are only grieving after a child who will soon forget you, as children do. You never give a thought to *my* despair; you don't know what love is; you have no love for me, and you will soon forget me, so perhaps you will never come back again."

"Yes, I shall come back, Landry—I take God to witness that I shall come back in a year, or at most two years, and I shall be so far from forgetting you, that I shall never have another friend or lover but you."

"It may be true that you will never have another friend, for you will never find one who will yield to you as I have done, but I don't know about another lover; who can be sure of that?"

"I can answer for it."

"You don't know anything about it yourself, Fadette. You have never loved, and when you do find out what love is, you will think no more of your poor Landry. Ah, if you had only loved me as I love you, you would never leave me like this!"

"Do you think so, Landry?" said little Fadette, looking at him sadly and thoughtfully. "Perhaps you don't know what you are saying. I believe that I should do far more for love than I should for friendship."

"Ah, well, if you were really actuated by love, I should not feel so distressed. Ah, yes! Fanchon, if I thought you were going away for love's sake, I believe that I should be almost happy, in the midst of all my grief. I should have faith in your promises and hope for the future. I should be as brave as you are—I should indeed. But it is not love—you have told me so many a time, and your calm behaviour toward me has proved the truth of what you say."

" So you think it is not love?" said little Fadette. "You are quite sure of that?"

And as she looked at him, her eyes filled with tears which rolled down her cheeks, and her lips wore a strange smile.

"Ah, good Lord!" cried Landry, clasping her in his arms, "if I have made a mistake!"

"You have indeed made a mistake," answered little Fadette, between smiles and tears. "I know that ever since she was thirteen years old, poor Cricket has set her heart on Landry and on no one else. I know that when she followed him about the fields and roads, talking nonsense to him, and teasing him to make him take some notice of her, she did not know what she was doing or what it was that drew her to him. I know that when she set out one day to look for Sylvinet—knowing that Landry was in trouble—and found him sitting beside the river, lost in thought, with a little lamb on his lap, she tried a little witchcraft on Landry so that he might be forced to owe her a debt of gratitude. I know, too, that when she abused him at the Roulettes ford, it was because she was angry and hurt that he had never spoken to her since that day. I know that when she was crying in the Chaumois road, it was because she was sorry for having offended him. I know that when she asked him to dance with her, it was because she was wild about him, and was in hopes of pleasing him by her pretty dancing. I know, too, that when he wanted to kiss her, and she refused, when he made love to her, and she answered him by talking of friendship, it was because she feared to forfeit his love if she yielded too quickly. In short, I know that if she is breaking her heart by going away, it is in the hope that she may return worthy of him in the opinion of everybody, and fit to be his wife, without bringing distress and mortification on his family."

When Landry heard this, he thought he should lose his wits altogether. He laughed, he cried, he shouted. He kissed Fanchon's hands, he kissed her dress, he would have kissed her feet, had she allowed him to do so, but she raised him up and gave him a true love kiss which was almost the death of him, for it was the first he had ever received from her or anyone else. He fell, half fainting, by the roadside; she picked up her bundle, blushing and agitated as she was, and ran off, forbidding him to follow her, and vowing that she would come back again.

XXX

Chapter 30

Landry submitted, and returned to the vintage, much surprised to find that he was not so unhappy as he had expected to be, for it is very comforting to know that one's love is returned, and when one's affection is great, one's faith is equally so. He was so surprised and so delighted that he could not help telling young Caillaud, who was also surprised and admired little Fadette for the prudence she had shown in behaving herself with such strength of mind and dignity, during all the time that Landry and she had been in love with each other.

"I am glad to see," said he, "that this girl has so much character, for I have never had a bad opinion of her, and I must acknowledge that if she had ever taken any notice of me, I should have fancied her. She has such fine eyes that I have always thought her more pretty than ugly, and for some time past anybody could see plainly enough that she was getting more attractive every day if she had cared to make herself agreeable. But she cared for nobody but you, Landry, and was satisfied as long as others did not dislike her. She never sought any admiration but yours, and I tell you that is the kind of woman that suits me. I have known her from a child, and have always thought her good-hearted, and, if everybody who knows her should give you his honest opinion, you would find the verdict in her favour. But that's the way of the world! Just let two or three people set after anybody, and all the rest join in the chase—throw stones, and try their best to ruin the person's reputation, and for no reason whatever, unless it may be for the pleasure they take in crushing one who is defenceless."

Landry took great comfort in listening to young Caillaud's moralizing, and from that time on they became warm friends, and it was quite a consolation to be able to talk to him about his woes. So one day Landry said to him, "Don't waste another thought on Madelon, my dear Caillaud. You are no older than I am, and you have plenty of time to think about getting married. Now, I have a little sister Nanette, who is as pretty as a picture, well brought up, sweet-tempered—a real little darling—and she will soon be sixteen. Come and see us a little oftener! My father thinks a good deal of you, and when you get acquainted with Nanette, you will see that you couldn't do better than to become my brother-in-law."

"Upon my word, I agree with you," answered Caillaud, "and if the girl is not already engaged, I will call at your house every Sunday evening."

The evening that Fanchon Fadet left, Landry made up his mind to go and tell his father how well the girl had behaved whom he had so misjudged, and, at the same time, to offer him his submission for the present, though he would not commit himself for the future. His heart beat fast as he passed Mother Fadet's house, but he summoned all his courage, thinking to himself that if Fadette had not gone away, it might have been a long time before he could have discovered that he was so fortunate as to have won her heart. And he saw Mother Fanchette, who was Fanchon's relative and godmother, and who had come to take her place in caring for the old woman and the child. She was sitting in the doorway, with the Grasshopper on her lap. Poor Jeanet was crying and did not want to go to bed, because his dear Fanchon had not yet come in, said he, and he wanted her to hear him say his prayers and tuck him in. Mother Fanchette did her best to comfort him, and Landry was glad to hear her speak so kindly and gently to him. But as soon as the Grasshopper caught sight of Landry, he slipped away from Mother Fanchette, at the risk of leaving one of his claws behind, and ran and threw his arms around Landry's legs, hugging him and asking him all sorts of questions, and begging him to bring back his dear Fanchon. Landry took him in his arms and did his best to soothe him, though he could not help shedding tears himself. He tried to make him take a bunch of fine grapes which he was carrying to Mother Barbeau from Mother Caillaud, but Jeanet, who was generally greedy enough, would not accept anything, nor obey Mother Fanchette, till Landry promised him, with a sigh, to go and look for his Fanchon.

Father Barbeau was not prepared for this step on the part of Fadette. He was pleased, but could not help regretting the course she had taken, for he was a just and kind-hearted man. "I am sorry, Landry, that you had not the strength of will to give up going to see her. If you had done your duty, she would not have been obliged to leave home. God grant that the poor child may do well in her new position and that her grandmother and her little brother may not suffer by her absence, for though there are a good many who speak ill of her, there are some who take her part, and say that she was very kind to her family, and did a great deal for them. We shall soon see whether the ugly stories they tell about her are true or not, and we'll stand up for her as we ought. If unfortunately, they should turn out to be true, and you, Landry, are the guilty party, we will come to her assistance, and not allow her to suffer. All I ask of you, Landry, is that you will never marry her."

"Father," said Landry, "you and I do not take the same view of the matter. If I were guilty of the offence to which you allude, I should, on the contrary, ask your permission to marry her. But as little Fadette is as innocent as my sister Nanette, I only ask you to forgive me now for giving you so much trouble. We will talk about her later on, as you promised me."

Father Barbeau was obliged to yield to these conditions and let the subject drop for the present. He was too prudent to attempt to hurry up matters, and so was forced to rest content with the progress he had made.

From that time on, nothing was said about Fadette at the Twinnery, for Landry turned red and then pale when anybody happened to mention her name in his presence, and it was easy enough to see that he was as fond of her as ever.

XXXI

Chapter 31

At first, Sylvinet was selfish enough to feel glad that Fadette had gone away, and flattered himself that now Landry would care for nobody but him and that nobody would ever again take his place. But this did not turn out to be the case. Landry certainly loved Sylvinet better than anybody in the world after Fanchon, but he could not long be happy in his society, for Sylvinet would not make an effort to overcome his dislike of Fanchon. As soon as Landry began to talk to him about her, and tried to win him over to her side, Sylvinet became very much agitated and reproached him because he persisted in worrying his father and mother and distressing him. So Landry said no more to him about it, but as he felt as if he must talk to someone, he divided his time between young Caillaud and little Jeanet. He took the child out walking with him, and heard his catechism, and taught him and comforted him as well as he could.

When people met him with the child, they would have ridiculed him had they dared. But in addition to the fact that Landry never allowed anybody to ridicule him on any subject, he was more proud than ashamed of his championship of Fanchon Fadet's brother, and this was his way of answering those who insisted that Father Barbeau had been clever enough to put an end to his love-affair in short order. Sylvinet found that his brother was still somewhat alienated from him, and was jealous of both young Caillaud and little Jeanet. He saw also that his sister Nanette, who had all along comforted and cheered him with her tender caresses and loving ways, was beginning to take pleasure in the society of young Caillaud, whose attention met with the approval of both families. Poor Sylvinet, who wished to reign supreme in the affections of those whom he loved, became strangely languid and melancholy, and so gloomy and low-spirited that nothing could rouse him. He no longer laughed, he took no interest in anything; he had grown so weak and feeble that he was hardly able to work. At last, they began to be alarmed about him, for his fever was almost incessant, and when it was a little higher than usual, he was flighty in his talk and wounded his parents' feelings. He insisted that nobody loved him, though he had been more spoiled and petted than any member of the family. He wished that he could die, and said that he was of no use to anybody, that his friends treated him kindly because they pitied him, but that he was a burden to his parents, and it would be a great mercy to them if God would take him away.

Sometimes Father Barbeau reproved the boy severely when he heard him talk in such an un-Christian way, but it did no good. Then Father Barbeau would entreat him, with tears, to believe that he loved him. This was worse still. Sylvinet cried, repented, and asked forgiveness of his father, his mother, his twin brother, and the whole family, but the fever always came back with renewed force, from having given way to his morbid feelings.

They consulted the doctors again. They had not much advice to give but seemed to think that all the trouble arose from the fact that he was a twin, and that one or the other of them—probably the weaker one—would certainly die. So they consulted the bath woman at Clavières, who was the best nurse in the district, now that Mother Sagette was dead and Mother Fadet was getting childish. This clever woman told Mother Barbeau, "The only thing which can save your child is falling in love with some girl."

"And he can't bear girls," said Mother Barbeau. "I have never seen a boy so shy and retiring, and from the time that his twin brother took it into his head to fall in love, Sylvinet hasn't had a good word for any girl of our acquaintance. He abuses them all because one of them—and, unfortunately, not one of the best—stole his brother's heart away from him."

"Well," said the nurse, who was very skilful in diseases of both mind and body, "when your son Sylvinet does fall in love with a woman, he will love her much more warmly than he does his brother. Mark my words. His heart is too full of love, and as he has always bestowed it all on his brother, he has almost forgotten his sex and has thus sinned against the law of God, which ordains that a man should cherish his wife more than father or mother, sister or brother. But cheer up! He must soon listen to the voice of nature, however backwards he may be. Don't refuse to let him marry the woman whom he may fancy, no matter how poor and ugly and disagreeable she may be, for, as far as I can judge, he will love but once. His heart is too faithful ever to change, and if it requires a great miracle of nature to wean him from his twin, it must be a still greater one to make him forget the woman whom he may come to love even more than he does his brother."

Father Barbeau was much impressed by the opinion of the nurse, and he tried to get Sylvinet to visit at those houses where there were good and pretty girls of marriageable age. But, though Sylvinet was a handsome young fellow, and had pleasant manners, he looked so sad and so indifferent that the girls did not fancy him. They would not make any advances to him, and he was so shy that he imagined that he hated them, when, in fact, he was only afraid of them.

Father Caillaud, who was the most intimate friend and adviser of the family, then had another piece of advice to offer.

"I have always told you," said he, "that absence is the best cure. Just look at Landry! He was distracted about little Fadette, and now that she has gone away, he is none the worse in mind or body. He doesn't even seem as sad as he used to be, for we noticed how he looked and wondered what could be the matter. Now he seems quite sensible and resigned. It would be the same with Sylvinet if he did not see his brother for five or six months. I'll tell you how you can separate them without making any trouble. My La Priche farm is doing well, but the property which I own over toward Arton is in very poor condition, for my tenant has been ill for about a year and isn't getting any better. I don't want to turn him out, for he is an honest man, but if I could send him a good assistant he would soon improve, for there is nothing the matter with him but hard work and anxiety. If you are agreed, I will send Landry over to spend the rest of the season on my property. We needn't let Sylvinet know how long he will be gone. On the contrary, we will tell him that Landry will be gone a week. Then after a week has passed, we'll say that he will be gone another week—and so on, till he gets accustomed to being separated from him. Now just follow my advice, instead of humouring the whims of a spoiled child who has got the upper hand of you."

Father Barbeau was disposed to follow this advice, but Mother Barbeau was afraid. It seemed to her that it would be a death-blow to Sylvinet. So they agreed to make a compromise; she begged that Landry might first be kept at home for a fortnight, to see if his brother would not get well by having him with him all the time. But if Sylvinet got worse, she would consent to take the advice of Father Caillaud.

And so Landry came to stay the allotted time at the Twinnery—greatly to his satisfaction—and they made an excuse that his father needed him to help finish threshing the wheat, as Sylvinet was no longer able to help him work. Landry was as kind as possible to his brother and did his best to please him. He stayed with him continually; he slept in the same bed; he took care of him as if he had been a little child. The first day, Sylvinet was in very good spirits, but the second he took it into his head that Landry was tired of him, and Landry could not make him believe otherwise. The third day, Sylvinet got angry because the Grasshopper came to see Landry, and Landry had not the heart to send him away. Finally, at the end of the week, they had to give it up, for Sylvinet became more and more unreasonable and exacting, and was jealous of his own shadow. Then they determined to try Father Caillaud's plan, and though Landry, who was so fond of his native place, his work, his family, and that of his employer, did not at all fancy going to Arton among strangers, he was perfectly willing to do what they proposed with the hope of benefiting his brother.

XXXII

~~~~~~~

Chapter 32

The first day, Sylvinet nearly died, but the second he was calmer, and the third the fever had left him. First, he became resigned, then he mustered up a little spirit, and by the time the first week had passed, it was plain to be seen that his brother's absence had done him good. A secret feeling of jealousy suggested a reason for being almost glad that Landry had gone away. "At any rate," thought he, "he doesn't know anybody over there, and he can't make new friends at once. He will be a little homesick, and he'll think of me, and wish he could see me. When he comes back, he'll love me better than ever."

Landry had been gone for about three months, and little Fadette almost a year, when she unexpectedly returned, because her grandmother had had a stroke of paralysis. She nursed her carefully and tenderly, but age is an incurable disease, and in about a fortnight Mother Fadet suddenly died. Three days afterwards, little Fadette, having buried the poor old woman, put the house in order, undressed her little brother and put him to bed, and kissed her godmother, who had retired to rest in another room, sat sadly enough beside her little fire, which threw out but little light, and listened to the cricket on the hearth, which seemed to say to her:

"Fay, fay, my little fay,
Take thy torch and haste away;
Here's my cap and here's my cloak,
And here's a mate for fairy folk."

The rain pattered against the windowpane, freezing as it fell, and Fanchon was thinking of her lover when there came a knock at the door and a voice said, "Fanchon Fadet, are you there, and do you recognize me?"

It did not take her long to open the door, and great was her delight to find herself in Landry's arms. He had heard of her grandmother's illness and her own return. He could not resist the temptation to come and see her, and he came at night, intending to go away at daybreak. So they spent the night talking at the fireside, but very soberly and seriously, for little Fadette reminded Landry that the bed on which her grandmother had died was scarcely cold yet, and it was neither the time nor the place to give themselves up to their own delight at seeing each other once more. But still, despite their good resolutions, they could not help feeling very happy to be together again and to assure themselves that they loved each other more than ever. As the day began to dawn, however, Landry's courage failed him, and he begged Fanchon to hide him in her garret so that he might see her again the next night. But, as usual, she brought him to his senses. She told him that they would not be separated much longer, for she had made up her mind to remain at home.

"I have my reasons for that, which I will tell you later," said she, "and which shall not stand in the way of our marrying someday. Go and finish the work which your master has given you to do, for, from what my godmother tells me, it is necessary for your brother's recovery that he should not see you for some time to come."

"That is the only reason which could induce me to leave you," answered Landry, "for my poor twin has caused me a good deal of anxiety, and I am afraid that I shall still suffer on his account. You are so clever, Fanchonette, you ought to be able to think of some way of curing him."

"I don't know any other way than to reason with him," answered she, "for it is his mind which is injuring his body, and whoever could cure one, would cure the other. But he has such a dislike to me that I shall never have an opportunity to talk to him, and try to comfort him."

"But you are so clever, Fadette—you talk so well, and you have such a talent for persuading anybody to think just what you please when you choose to take the trouble, that if you could only talk to him for one hour, it would have an effect on him. Try it, I beg of you! Don't mind his pride and ill-humour! Make him listen to you. Make this effort for my sake, my dear Fanchon, and for the sake of our love also, for my brother's opposition is not the least of our troubles."

So Fanchon gave him her promise, and they parted, after mutual assurances of love and fidelity.

XXXIII

Chapter 33

Nobody in the neighbourhood knew that Landry had been home. If Sylvinet had happened to hear of it, he would have fallen ill again, and would never have forgiven Landry for coming to see Fadette and not himself.

Two days afterwards, little Fadette dressed very neatly, for she was no longer penniless, and her mourning gown was of fine serge. She walked through La Cosse, and as she had grown a great deal, those who saw her pass did not at first recognize her. She had grown to be much better looking while she had been away in the city. Good food and lodging had improved her complexion, she was as plump as a girl of her age ought to be, and there was no longer any danger of her being mistaken for a boy in disguise, for she had a very pretty, graceful figure. Love had given her whole person that indescribable charm which nobody can fail to remark. In short, if she were not the prettiest girl in the world, as Landry imagined her to be, she was the most winning and the freshest girl in the neighbourhood and had the most attractive face and figure.

She had a basket on her arm, and she stopped at the Twinnery, where she asked to see Father Barbeau. Sylvinet was the first to see her, and he was so annoyed at meeting her that he turned his back. But she asked him so politely where his father was, that he was obliged to answer her and take her to the barn, where Father Barbeau was busy at some carpentering work. Fadette having asked to see him alone so that she might have a private conversation with him, he shut the barn door and told her that he was ready to hear what she had to say to him.

Little Fadette did not allow herself to be discouraged by Father Barbeau's coldness. She seated herself on a bundle of straw, he sat down on another, and she began.

"Father Barbeau, though my grandmother, who is dead and gone, had a great dislike for you, and you have a grudge against me, it is nevertheless true that I have always known that you are the most honourable and upright man in this part of the country. There are no two opinions on that subject, and my grandmother herself, while she accused you of being proud, did you that justice. Besides that, your son Landry and I have been friends for a long time, as you know. He has often talked to me about you, and I know from him, even better than from others, what a good man you are. That is the reason I have come to ask a favour of you and to take you into my confidence."

"Go on, Fadette," said Father Barbeau. "I have never yet refused to help anybody, and if it is anything which my conscience does not forbid, you may rely upon my doing what I can for you."

"It is this," said Fadette, lifting her basket, and setting it down at Father Barbeau's feet. "My grandmother, when she was alive, earned more money than you would suppose possible by giving advice and by the sale of her remedies, and, as she hardly spent anything, and never made any investments, of course, nobody suspected what she had in an old hole in her cellar, which she often pointed out to me, and said, "After I am gone, you will find in there all that I have to leave you. It belongs to you and your brother, and if you are a little pinched now, you will be all the richer some day or other. But don't let the lawyers get hold of it, for they'd eat it all up in costs. Keep it when you get it—hide it away as long as you live, so that you may not come to want in your old age.

"After my poor grandmother was buried, I did as she had told me. I took the key to the cellar and pried out the bricks in the wall, just where she had shown me. There I found what I have brought you in this basket, Father Barbeau, and I beg of you to invest it as you see fit, after doing whatever the law may demand, and avoiding the heavy expenses of which I am afraid."

"I am much obliged to you for the confidence you have expressed in me, Fadette," said Father Barbeau, without looking into the basket, though he felt considerable curiosity as to its contents, "but I have no right to take charge of your money, or to manage your affairs. I am not your guardian. Your grandmother must have left a will."

"She did not leave a will, but my mother is my legal guardian. Now, you know it is a long time since I have heard anything about her, and I don't know whether she is dead or alive, poor thing. My nearest relative after her, is my godmother Fanchette, who is a good, honest woman, but quite incapable of managing my property, or even indeed of keeping it safely locked up. She would be sure to talk about it and show it to everybody, and I should be afraid that she would make poor investments, or that by allowing so many inquisitive people to handle it, a good deal of it might be taken without her knowledge. My poor, dear godmother doesn't even know how to count it."

"So it is a considerable sum?" asked Father Barbeau, his eyes fastened, despite himself, on the cover of the basket. He lifted it by the handle to ascertain its weight. He was amazed to find it so heavy, and said, " If it is in small coin, a load for a horse wouldn't amount to much."

Little Fadette, who had a keen sense of humour, was much amused at his evident curiosity about the contents of the basket. She made a motion as if to open it, but Father Barbeau considered it beneath his dignity to allow her to do so.

"It is none of my business," said he, "and as I can't take charge of your money, I have no right to know anything about your affairs."

"But, Father Barbeau, you will, at least, do me this one little service! I can't count above a hundred much better than my godmother. Besides, I don't know the value of all the coins, old and new, and you are the only one I can trust to tell me whether I am rich or poor and to give me the exact amount of my property."

"Well, let's see, then," said Father Barbeau, who could hold out no longer. "That's no great favour to ask, and I ought not to refuse you."

Then Fadette quickly raised the two lids of the basket and

took out two big bags, each of which contained two thousand francs in crown pieces.

"Well, that's very nice," said Father Barbeau. "There is a little dowry, which will bring you a suitor or two."

"That isn't all," said Fadette, "there is some more at the bottom of the basket, though I don't know how much it is."

And she drew out an eel-skin purse, which she emptied into Father Barbeau's hat. There were a hundred gold louis—evidently old coins—which made the honest man open his eyes. When he had counted them, and put them back in the eel skin, she took out another just like it, and then a third, and a fourth, and finally, in gold, silver, and small coin, there was not much less than forty thousand francs in the basket.

That was about one-third more than the value of all Father Barbeau's buildings, and, as country people never have much ready money, he had never seen so large a sum in his life.

However honest and disinterested a peasant may be, nobody can say of him that he hates the sight of money, and so Father Barbeau felt the drops of perspiration start out on his forehead, for a moment.

When he had done counting, he said, "You lack only twenty-two crowns of having forty thousand francs, and your share of the property is about two thousand pistoles in ready money. That makes you the greatest heiress in these parts, Fadette, and your brother, the Grasshopper, may stay lame and sickly all his life; he can take a carriage to look after his property. You may consider yourself fortunate, for you need only let it be known that you are rich if you want to get a good husband."

"I am in no hurry," said Fadette, "and I must beg you, on the contrary, not to let anybody know how rich I am, Father Barbeau. Ugly as I am, I don't want to be married for my money, but for my good heart and my fair name. And as I have had a bad reputation in this part of the country, I mean to stay here sometime, to prove that I don't deserve it."

"As for your ugliness, Fadette," said Father Barbeau, raising his eyes, which had been fastened on the basket, "I can tell you, in sober earnest, that you have got bravely over it, and have improved so much since you went to the city that you will pass for a very nice-looking girl nowadays. And as for your bad name, if, as I hope is the case, you do not deserve it, I approve of your idea of waiting awhile before you let it be known that you are rich, for there are plenty of men who would want to marry you for your money, without feeling for you the regard which a woman should demand from her husband.

"Now as for the money which you wish to deposit with me, it would be contrary to law for me to take it and might expose me, later on, to false suspicions and accusations, for there are plenty of scandal-mongers about. Besides, supposing you had a right to dispose of what belongs to you, you have no authority over the property of your brother, who is a minor. All that I can do will be to ask advice for you, without mentioning your name. Then I will let you know how to invest your legacy and your brother's, so that it will be safe, without letting it fall into the hands of pettifoggers, who are not all to be trusted.

Take it away, then, and hide it again till I can give you an answer. I place myself at your disposal if you need me, to testify before the attorneys of your co-heir, as to the amount of the sum which we have just been counting, and which I am going to write down in the corner of my barn so that I shall not forget it."

All that Fadette wanted was that Father Barbeau should know just how matters stood. If she was rather glad to let him know that she was rich, it was only because now he could no longer accuse her of setting her cap for Landry.

XXXIV

❦

Chapter 34

Father Barbeau, seeing how prudent and clever she was, was not in such haste to deposit and invest her money, as he was to make inquiries as to the reputation she had borne at Château Meillant, where she had spent the year of her absence. Though her large dowry was very tempting and made him feel inclined to overlook her unfortunate connections, it was quite a different matter when the honour of the girl he hoped to call his daughter-in-law was in question. So he went in person to Château Meillant and instituted the strictest inquiries. He learned not only that it was false that Fadette had gone there to give birth to a child, but also that she had conducted herself so well that there was absolutely nothing to be said to her disadvantage. She had been in the service of a nun of a noble family, who had taken pleasure in making a companion of her, instead of a servant, having found her so well-behaved, so sensible, and so well-mannered. She regretted losing her and said that she was a lovely Christian character, frank, neat, careful, and so amiable in disposition that she never expected to find another like her.

As this old lady was quite wealthy, she was interested in many charities, and Fadette had been of great service to her in caring for the sick and in compounding medicines, and her mistress had taught her how to prepare several valuable secret remedies, which she had learned in her convent before the Revolution.

Father Barbeau was much pleased, and he came back to La Cosse determined to sift the matter to the bottom. He called his family together and charged his older children, his brothers, and all his relatives, to inquire closely into Fadette's mode of life since she had arrived at years of discretion, so that, if all the gossip about her had arisen merely from some childish piece of folly, they might set it at nought; but if, on the contrary, anybody could claim to have seen her commit an actual misdemeanour or knew her to be guilty of any act of impropriety, he should enforce his order that Landry should have nothing further to do with her. The investigation was conducted with great prudence, as he had desired, and there was no mention made of the dowry, for he had not even told his wife about that.

All this time, Fadette was living a very retired life in her little house, which remained unchanged, excepting that it was kept so clean that you could have seen your face in the simple furniture.

She dressed her little Grasshopper neatly and made by degrees so great a change for the better in their food, that the effect was soon apparent on the child. His health improved greatly, and he soon became as healthy as one could wish. His disposition altered under the influence of happiness, and now that his grandmother was no longer there to threaten him, and nag at him, and as he met with nothing but caresses, kind words, and good treatment, he grew to be a nice little boy, full of quaint and pretty fancies, so that nobody could think of disliking him, despite his limp and his little snub nose.

In addition to that, there was so marked a change in the person and habits of Fanchon Fadet, that all the ugly stories about her were forgotten, and more than one young fellow, as he saw her pass by with her light step and graceful carriage, wished that her mourning were at an end so that he might pay court to her, and invite her to dance.

Sylvinet Barbeau was the only one who still adhered to his former opinion of her. He saw plainly enough that something was brewing in his family concerning her, for his father could not resist speaking of her now and then, and whenever some old lie about her was proved to be false, he congratulated himself on Landry's account, saying that he could not bear to have his son accused of ruining an innocent young girl.

Landry's approaching return began also to be talked about, and Father Barbeau seemed to be anxious that Father Caillaud should agree to it. At last, Sylvinet saw that all opposition to Landry's love-affair was about to be withdrawn, and he became as wretched as ever. Public opinion, which varies with the wind, had for some time past been in favour of Fadette; nobody knew that she was rich, but she made friends, and for that very reason Sylvinet disliked her all the more, for she seemed to him to be a rival for Landry's affections.

Once in a while, Father Barbeau let slip in his presence a word about marriage, saying that the twins would soon be old enough to be thinking of settling themselves. Sylvinet had never been able to think of Landry's getting married without the greatest distress, and it seemed to him as if it would be a death-blow to their affection and companionship. His fever returned, and his mother sent for the doctors once more.

One day she met Mother Fanchette, who, hearing how anxious she was, asked her why she sent so far for advice and spent so much money when she had at her very door a more skilful doctor than any in the country—one who did not wish to practise for money as her grandmother had done, but only for the love of God and of her neighbour. Then she mentioned little Fadette.

Mother Barbeau spoke of it to her husband, who made no objection. He told her that Fadette had a great reputation in Château Meillant for her skill in healing and that people came from far and near to consult her and her mistress. So Mother Barbeau begged Fadette to come and see Sylvinet, who was now ill in bed and requested her to do what she could for him.

Fanchon had more than once tried to find an opportunity of speaking to him, following her promise to Landry, but he had always avoided her.

So she did not wait to be urged but went at once to see the poor twin. She found him in a feverish sleep and asked to be left alone with him. As it is customary for doctresses to work their cures in secret, there was no objection made, and nobody remained in the room.

The first thing Fadette did was to lay her hand on his, which rested on the edge of the bed. She did it so gently, however, that he was not aware of it, though his sleep was so light that he woke if a fly buzzed in the room. Sylvinet's hand was hot as fire, and it became hotter still as little Fadette continued to hold it in hers. He seemed agitated but did not try to withdraw his hand. Then Fadette placed her other hand on his forehead, as gently as before, and he became still more restless. But, little by little, he calmed down, and she could feel her patient's head and hand grow cooler from minute to minute. He was soon sleeping as quietly as a little child. She remained beside him till she saw that he was about to wake, and then she slipped behind his curtain, and left the room and the house, saying to Mother Barbeau, as she passed, "Go and see your son, and give him something to eat, for his fever is gone, and above everything, don't talk to him about me, if you want me to cure him. I will come back this evening, at the hour when you say his disease is at its height, and I will try to break this raging fever again."

XXXV

⟨✹⟩

Chapter 35

Mother Barbeau was much astonished to see Sylvinet free from fever, and she hastened to give him something to eat, which he took with some appetite. As his fever had lasted six days without a break, and he had not been able to take anything, the family were enthusiastic over Fadette's skill, for, without waking him up or giving him anything to drink, she had already benefited him so much, solely by the aid of her spells, or so it seemed to them.

Toward evening, the fever returned, and his temperature was very high. Sylvinet was dozing and his mind was wandering, and when he woke, he was afraid of those who stood around his bed.

Fadette came again, and, as in the morning, remained alone with him for nearly an hour, and the only magic she used was to hold his hands and head in a soft clasp and to breathe on his hot cheeks with her cool, fresh breath.

His fever and delirium vanished as in the morning, and when she left, still requesting that he should not be told that she had been there, they found him sleeping quietly—his face no longer flushed—and apparently completely restored to health. I do not know where Fadette had picked up this idea. She had found out, partly by chance and partly by experience, that when her little brother Jeanet was at the point of death she had been able to relieve him a dozen times or more, by simply cooling him with her hands and breath, and warming him in the same way, when the burning fever was preceded by chills. She believed that the affection and good-will of a person in sound health, and the laying on of a hand, full of vitality and free from any taint of sin, has the power to banish disease, provided that the person is endowed with a certain temperament, and has firm faith in God's goodness. She engaged in silent prayer while her hands rested on the patient. This treatment—which she was now trying on Sylvinet, and which was the same she had given her little brother—she would not have been willing to administer to anyone in whom she was not greatly interested, for she believed that its chief efficacy lay in the love in her heart, which she offered as a sacrifice to the Lord, and without which He would not have granted her power to relieve the patient.

And so, while Fadette was charming away Sylvinet's fever, she repeated the same prayer which she had made beside her sick brother. "O God, let my health pass out of my body into this suffering body, and as our dear Saviour offered up His life to redeem the souls of all mankind, if it be Thy will to take away my life and bestow it upon this sick person, I give it into Thy hands. I gladly yield it in exchange for the recovery of him for whom

198 - GEORGE SAND

I am praying." Little Fadette had thought of making this prayer at her grandmother's deathbed, but she did not venture, for it seemed to her that the old woman's life was dying out in body and soul, as the result of old age, and following that natural law which God Himself has established. So Fadette, who, as you see, trusted more to piety than to witchcraft in working her charms, feared to displease Him by asking for anything which He grants to other Christians only as a special miracle. Whether the remedy had any special virtue of its own or not, one thing is certain, in three days Sylvinet had recovered from his fever, and would never have known how his cure was brought about, if, on her last visit, he had not happened to wake a little sooner than usual, and caught sight of her bending over him, and softly withdrawing her hands. At first, he thought that it was a vision and closed his eyes to avoid the sight of her. But afterwards when he asked his mother whether Fadette had not held his hand and felt his pulse, Mother Barbeau, to whom her husband had at last given a hint of his plans, and who was anxious that Sylvinet should overcome his dislike to Fanchon, answered that she had been there every morning and evening for the last three days, and, by some secret process, had broken his fever in the most miraculous way.

Sylvinet did not seem to believe what she said. He said that the fever had left him of its own accord and that Fadette's spells and incantations were all silly nonsense. He improved so much in the course of the next few days that Father Barbeau thought best to speak to him as to the possibility of his brother's marriage, but without mentioning the name of the wife he had in view for him.

"You need not hide the name of the bride you intend to give

him," answered Sylvinet. "I know well enough that it is Fadette, who has cast a spell over you all."

In fact, Father Barbeau's private inquiries into Fadette's character had resulted so much to her advantage, that he no longer hesitated, and was quite eager to send for Landry to come home. The only fear he now had was the jealousy of his twin brother, and he tried to cure him of this weakness by telling him that his brother would never be happy without Fadette. But Sylvinet answered, "Do just as you think best; my brother must be happy, whatever happens!"

But they did not dare take any steps in the matter as yet, for Sylvinet's fever returned as soon as he seemed to have given up his opposition.

XXXVI

Chapter 36

Father Barbeau, however, was afraid that Fadette might cherish some resentment against him for his past injustice, and that having become accustomed to Landry's absence, she might have taken up with some other admirer. When she came to the Twinnery to look after Sylvinet, he had tried to speak to her about Landry, but she pretended not to understand him, and he was quite puzzled as to what course to take.

At last, one morning, he made up his mind to go and see Fadette.

"Fanchon Fadet," said he, "I have come to ask you a question, and I beg you to answer me honestly and truly. Had you any idea before your grandmother's death that she would leave you so much property?"

"Yes, Father Barbeau," answered Fadette, "I had some idea of it, for I had often seen her counting gold and silver and I never saw her spend anything but copper, and also because she often said to me when the other girls made fun of my rags, 'Don't you worry about that, little one—you will have more money than any of them someday, and you can dress in silk from head to foot if you choose to do so."

"As far as I am concerned, Father Barbeau," said Fadette, "as I always wanted to be loved for the sake of my fine eyes, which is the only beauty I am supposed to possess, I was not so silly as to tell Landry that all my charms were tied up in eel-skin bags, and yet I might have ventured to let him know, for Landry's love is so true and so devoted that it would have made no difference to him whether I was rich or poor."

"And since your grandmother's death, dear Fanchon," continued Father Barbeau, "can you give me your word of honour that Landry has not heard of the state of the case, from you or anyone else?"

"I can," said Fadette. "I swear to you by my love for my Maker, that you are the only person in the world besides myself who knows anything about it."

"And do you think that Landry is still in love with you, Fanchon? Have you received any token of his fidelity to you since your grandmother's death?"

"I have received the best of assurances," answered she, "for I must tell you that he came to see me three days after my grandmother died and that he swore he would die of grief if I did not become his wife."

"And what answer did you give him, Fadette?"

"I am not called upon to answer that question, Father Barbeau, but I will do so if you wish it. I told him that there was time enough for us to think of getting married and that I did not like to receive attention from a man whose parents did not approve of me."

Fadette said this with an air of so much pride and indifference that Father Barbeau was quite disturbed.

"I have no right to question you, Fanchon Fadet," said he, "and I don't know whether you mean to make my son happy or unhappy for life, but I do know that he is head over heels in love with you, and if I were in your place and wanted to be loved for myself alone, I should think, 'Here's Landry Barbeau, who loved me when I was in rags when everybody despised me and when his own relations treated him as if he had committed a sin in caring for me. He thought me beautiful when everybody else thought me hopelessly ugly; he loved me despite all the troubles which that love brought upon him. He loved me as well when I was away as when we were together; in fact, he loves me so dearly that I cannot help trusting him and I will never marry anyone else.'"

"I've thought all that long ago, Father Barbeau," answered Fadette, "but I must tell you once more that I have the greatest objection to coming into a family which would be ashamed of me and which only give their consent out of pity."

"If that's all that stands in the way, you may set your mind at rest, Fanchon," said Father Barbeau, "for Landry's family has great regard for you and will be glad to welcome you. Don't fancy that we have changed our opinion because you are now rich. It was not your poverty which made us object, but the ugly stories which people told about you. If they had turned out to be well-founded, I should never have consented to call you my daughter-in-law, even if it had cost Landry his life. But I determined to find out the truth about these reports, so I went to Château Meillant for that very reason. I made very strict inquiries over there and in our own neighbourhood, and I am now convinced that they lied to me and that you are a good, honest girl, as Landry always persisted in declaring you to be. So now, Fanchon Fadet, I have come to ask you to marry my son, and if you say yes, he shall be here before the week is out."

This overture, which did not surprise her in the least, made Fadette feel very happy, but she took care not to let him see how delighted she was, for she wished that her future husband's family should continue to respect her. So she hesitated a moment. Then Father Barbeau said to her, "I see, my girl, that you still have a grudge against me and my family. Don't expect too many apologies from a man of my age. Just rely on my word when I tell you that we will all treat you with respect and affection. Father Barbeau has never yet deceived anybody, and you may believe what he tells you. Come now, will you give the kiss of peace to the guardian whom you chose for yourself or the father who wishes to adopt you?"

Fadette could hold out no longer. She threw her arms around Father Barbeau's neck, and his old heart rejoiced.

XXXVII

Chapter 37

The arrangements were soon made. The marriage was to take place as soon as the period of Fadette's mourning was over. There was nothing left to do but to send for Landry, but when Mother Barbeau came to see Fanchon that evening to give her a kiss and a blessing, she told her how Sylvinet had taken ill again as soon as he heard about his brother's approaching marriage, and she asked for a few days' delay so that he might have time to recover his health and spirits.

"You made a mistake, Mother Barbeau," said Fadette, "in not allowing Sylvinet to believe that it was a dream when he saw me at his bedside at the time when his fever left him. Now he will oppose his will to mine and I shall no longer have the power to relieve him in his sleep as I have done. I shall lose my influence over him and my presence may even make him worse."

"I don't think so," answered Mother Barbeau, "for just as soon as he was taken ill, a little while ago, he went to bed and said, 'Where is Fadette? I believe she helped me the last time. Won't she come back again?' And I told him that I would go for you, and he seemed pleased and even eager to have you come."

"I'll go," said Fadette, "but this time I shall try a different treatment, for, as I told you, the course I adopted when he was not aware of my presence will be useless now."

"And won't you take any medicines with you?" asked Mother Barbeau.

"No," said Fadette "there is not much the matter with his body. I must try and work on his mind. I am going to make an attempt to exert a moral influence over him, but I do not promise you that I shall be successful. One thing, however, I can promise you, and that is to wait patiently till Landry comes back, and not to ask you to send for him till we have done all in our power to restore his brother to health. Landry has so often begged me to try and help Sylvinet that I know he will approve, even though his return is postponed and his happiness delayed."

When Sylvinet saw Fadette standing beside his bed, he seemed annoyed and did not answer when she asked him how he felt. She tried to feel his pulse, but he drew his hand away and turned his face to the wall. Then Fadette made signs that she wanted to be left alone with him, and after everybody had gone out she extinguished the lamp, and let no other light enter the room except the rays of the moon, which was at its full. Then she came back to the bedside, and said to Sylvinet, in a tone of authority which he obeyed like a child, "Sylvinet, put both your hands in mine, and tell me the truth, for I did not come here for the sake of money, neither did I take the trouble to come here to treat you to have you behave so rudely and ungratefully to me. So now listen to what I ask you and take care how you answer me, for you cannot possibly deceive me."

"Ask me whatever you please, Fadette," answered the twin, quite taken aback at hearing little Fadette, who had always been such a madcap, speak to him so severely.

"Sylvain Barbeau," said she, "I believe you want to die."

Sylvain hesitated a moment before answering, and as Fadette kept a firm hold on his hand and made him feel the power of her will, he said rather shyly, "Wouldn't it be the best thing that could happen to me if I should die, when I can't help seeing that I am nothing but a burden and trouble to my family, on account of my bad health, and my—"

"Go on, Sylvain, don't keep anything back!"

"And my unhappy disposition, which I can't change," answered the twin, quite overcome.

"You had better say your bad heart," said Fadette, so sternly that he felt almost as much indignation as fear.

XXXVIII

Chapter 38

"Why do you accuse me of having a bad heart?" said he. "You insult me because you see that I have not the strength to defend myself."

"I told you the truth about yourself and I am going to tell you still more. I shall not take any pity on you because you are ill, for I know enough to see that it is not very serious, and if you are in any danger, it is of losing your mind, for you are doing your very best to make yourself crazy. You don't seem to have any idea what serious consequences your ill-temper and folly may produce."

"Say what you please about my folly," said Sylvinet, "but I do not deserve to be accused of ill-temper."

"Don't try to defend yourself," answered Fadette. "I know you better than you know yourself, Sylvain, and I tell you that weakness leads to deceit, and that has made you selfish and ungrateful."

"If you have such a poor opinion of me, Fanchon Fadet, it must be because my brother Landry has been talking ill of me, and you have found out how little he cares for me, for your only acquaintance with me must be through him."

"That's just what I expected you to say, Sylvain. I know that you could not talk long without complaining of your twin brother and finding fault with him, for the love you bear him is so foolish and immoderate that it easily degenerates into spitefulness and revenge. That shows me that you are not in your right mind and that you are not good. Well, I can tell you that Landry loves you ten times as much as you love him, for he never finds fault with you, no matter how you worry him, while you are forever reproaching him if he doesn't do just what you want him to do. How do you suppose that I can help seeing the difference between you and him? So the more Landry praised you, the worse opinion I had of you, for it seemed to me that you must have a very bad disposition to misunderstand so good a brother."

"And so you hate me, Fadette, don't you? I was sure I was not mistaken, and I knew you talked against me to my brother till he ceased to love me."

"That's just like you again, Master Sylvain, and I am glad that you lay the blame on me at last. Well, I must tell you that you are ill-natured and malicious since you wilfully misunderstand and insult a girl who has always tried to be good to you and has taken your part, though nobody knew better than she did that you did everything in your power to injure her. A girl who has many a time given up the only pleasure she had in the world—the pleasure of seeing Landry and of being with him—so that she might let Landry go to you and give you the happiness which she denied herself. And yet I was under no obligation to you. You have always been an enemy of mine, and as far back as I can remember I never saw a child so cruel and unfeeling to anybody as you have always been to me. I might have wished to take my revenge, and there were plenty of opportunities. If I have not availed myself of them, and if, without your knowledge, I have returned good for evil, it is because I believe it to be my duty to forgive my neighbour if I wish to please God. But you probably do not understand me when I speak to you of God, for you are an enemy to Him and your own salvation."

"I have allowed you to say a good many things to me, Fadette, but you are going too far when you accuse me of being a heathen."

"Didn't you tell me that you wanted to die? Do you call that the desire of a Christian?"

"I didn't say that Fadette—I said—" and Sylvinet stopped, startled at the recollection of his own words, which, now that Fadette had drawn his attention to them, really seemed impious.

But she would not let him alone and kept on remonstrating with him.

"It may be," said she, "that you did not mean all you said, for I am sure that you are not so anxious to die as you wish your family to suppose, so that they may all do just as you wish them to do, and that you may torment your mother, who is distressed to death, and your twin brother, who is innocent enough to believe that you would really like to put an end to yourself. But you can't deceive me, Sylvain. I believe that you are as much afraid to die as the rest of us, even more so, and that you enjoy playing upon the fears of those who love you. You like to see them yield to you even against their better judgment when you threaten to give up the ghost, and it must be very convenient and agreeable to have everybody give in to you at a word. That is the way you manage to rule your whole family. But as you use means of which God disapproves, and which are contrary to the natural order of things, He punishes you by making you even more wretched than you would be if you obeyed instead of commanding. And so you are weary of a life which has been made only too easy for you. Now let me tell you, Sylvain, what would have made a good, sensible boy of you. You should have had very severe parents, poverty, and scanty food, and plenty of whippings. If you had been brought up in the same school as myself and my brother Jeanet, you would be thankful for anything, instead of being as ungrateful as you are. Now, Sylvain, do not lay it all to your being a twin! I know that they have talked a great deal too much before you about that affection existing between twins, which is a law of nature, and which might perhaps cause your death if it were set at nought, and you thought that you were only carrying out your destiny when you bore this love to excess. But God is not so unjust as to single us out before our birth for an unhappy fate. He is not so cruel as to implant in us impulses which we cannot overcome, and you do Him wrong—superstitious creature that you are—by believing that the blood in your body has an irresistible power for evil, which your moral sense is incapable of combating. You can never make me believe that you could not have conquered your jealous disposition if you tried to do so, unless, indeed, your mind is unsettled. You do not make an effort to overcome it, because they pet you for this moral failing, and you are more guided by your whims than you are by your sense of duty."

Sylvinet did not reply and allowed Fadette to continue to reprove him unsparingly. He knew well enough that she was right in the main, and that in one respect only was she too severe. She professed to think that he had never made any effort to resist this evil propensity of his and that his selfishness was premeditated, whereas he had acted selfishly without knowing or intending it. This mortified and distressed him very much, and he would gladly have exonerated himself. She was quite aware that she had been exaggerating, and she had done it purposely so that he might be brought to a properly chastened frame of mind before she should proceed to comfort him and heal his wound. So she forced herself to speak sternly to him and to appear indignant, while her heart was so full of pity and tenderness that she was disgusted with the part she was playing and was more exhausted than he was.

XXXIX

Chapter 39

To tell the truth, Sylvinet was not half so ill as he seemed or as he wished them to believe, and chose to consider himself. When Fadette felt his pulse, she saw at once that he had but little fever, and·that, though he might be rather flighty, it was because his mind was not so strong as his body. So she thought that the best way of managing him was to make him afraid of her, and early the next morning she came to see him again. He had slept but little, but he was quiet and appeared to be exhausted. As soon as he saw her, he held out his hand, instead of snatching it away as he had done the night before.

"Why do you offer me your hand, Sylvain?" she inquired. "Do you want me to see whether you have any fever? I see by your face that it is all gone."

Sylvinet, ashamed at being obliged to draw back the hand which she did not seem inclined to take, said, "I want to shake hands with you, Fadette, and to thank you for all the trouble you have taken on my account."

"If that's the case, I will shake hands with you," said she, taking his hand and holding it in hers, for I never refuse an act of courtesy, and I don't believe you are so deceitful as to pretend to be friendly to me if you did not feel so."

Although this time, Sylvinet was wide awake, he was very glad indeed to allow his hand to rest in Fadette's, and he said to her very gently, "And yet you treated me very badly yesterday evening, Fanchon, and I don't see how it is that I am not angry with you. Indeed I feel much obliged to you for coming to see me after all the trouble I have given you."

Fadette sat down beside his bed and talked to him, but in a very different strain from her reproof of the night before. She was so kind, so gentle, and so affectionate, that Sylvinet was greatly relieved, and his pleasure was all the greater because he had believed that she was very angry with him. He wept freely, confessed his faults, and even begged her pardon and asked for her friendship with such good grace that it was plain to see that his heart was better than his head. She let him unburden himself, still scolding him a little, now and then, and when he tried to take away her hand, he held it fast, because it seemed to him that this hand had the power to cure him of both mental and bodily ailments. When she saw that he was in the right mood, she said, "Now I am going, Sylvain, and you must get up, for your fever is gone and you mustn't lie here, letting your mother wait on you and wasting her time sitting by your bedside. You must eat what your mother is preparing for you under my directions. It is meat, and I know that you say you have a horror of it and that you insist on eating nothing but vegetable messes, but no matter—you must force yourself to eat it and even if you do not like it you must not let her suspect it. Your mother will be gratified to see you eating substantial food and your dislike will decrease each time you make an effort to overcome it and finally, it will altogether disappear. You'll see if I am not telling you the truth. So now, goodbye, and don't let them come after me so early again, for I know you will not be ill any more unless you choose to be."

"You will come again this evening, won't you?" asked Sylvinet.

"I don't practise medicine for pay, Sylvain, and I have something better to do than to take care of you when you are not ill."

"You are right, Fadette, but you think that I only want to see you out of selfishness. It isn't that at all. I take great comfort in talking to you."

"Very well, you are not helpless, and you know where I live. You know that I am going to be your sister by marriage, as I am already in affection, so there will be no harm in your coming to see me."

"I shall come since you are willing that I should do so," said Sylvinet.

"So now, *au revoir*, Fadette. I am going to get up, though I have a bad headache from lying awake all night and grieving."

" I will try to cure your headache," said she, "but take care that it is the last, and remember, I order you to sleep soundly tonight."

She laid her hand on his forehead, and in about five minutes his head no longer ached, and he felt relieved and comfortable.

"I see that I did wrong not to allow you to help me, Fadette," said he, "for you are a great doctor and you can charm away sickness. All the others have done me harm by their medicines, and you have cured me just by laying your hands on me. I believe if I could have you always near me, I should not be ill again, and would never be so foolish and wicked as I have been. But tell me! You are not angry with me any more, are you? Will you rely on the promise I made you to do just as you tell me?"

"I shall rely on it, and if you don't change your mind, I shall be as fond of you as if you were my twin brother."

"If you really mean what you say, Fanchon, you would treat me like a brother, for twins do not speak to each other so formally."

"Well then, Sylvain, get up, eat your breakfast, talk, sleep, take a walk," said she, rising. "Those are my orders for today. Tomorrow you may go to work."

"And I shall go to see you."

"Very well," said she, and she left the room, giving him a look of pardon and affection, which at once inspired him with a desire to leave his bed of suffering and self-indulgence.

XL

Chapter 40

Mother Barbeau could not get over her amazement at the skill which Fadette had shown, and that evening she said to her husband, "Here is Sylvinet, feeling better than he has felt for the last six months. He has eaten everything I have given him today without any of his usual grimaces over it, and, what is still more remarkable, he speaks of Fadette as if she were the good Lord Himself. He can't say enough in her praise, and he is longing for his brother's return and marriage. It seems like an absolute miracle, and I don't know whether I am asleep or awake."

"Miracle or no miracle," said Father Barbeau, "the girl is very clever, and I think any family which gets her is lucky."

Three days afterwards, Sylvinet started off for Arton to bring his brother home. He had begged his father and Fadette to allow him, as a great favour, to be the first to tell Landry of his good fortune.

"All my happiness comes at once," said Landry, almost ready to die of joy, in Sylvinet's arms, "for you have come to bring me home, and seem as delighted as I am myself."

They came back together and did not linger on the way, as you may well imagine, and there never was a happier set of people than the family at the Twinnery, when they sat down to supper, with Fadette and Jeanet in their midst. Everything went smoothly for the next six months. Little Nanette became engaged to young Caillaud, who was Landry's best friend, outside his own family. It was decided that the two weddings should take place on the same day and at the same hour. Sylvinet had grown so fond of Fadette that he did nothing without consulting her, and she had as much influence over him as if she were really his sister. He was in excellent health, and there was no longer any talk of jealousy. If he still occasionally looked sad and was too much inclined to indulge in reverie, Fadette reproved him, and he at once began to smile and talk.

The two marriages took place on the same day and at the same Mass, and as both families were well-to-do, the wedding feast was so bountiful that Father Caillaud, who was always as sober and dignified as possible, made believe to be a little drunk the third day. There was nothing to dampen the enjoyment of Landry and the whole family, and, indeed, one might say, the whole neighbourhood, for the Barbeaus and Caillauds were rich, and Fadette had as much as both families together, so they extended their hospitality to everybody and gave away a good deal in charity. Fanchon was so kind-hearted that she wanted to return good for evil toward all those who had misjudged her. Indeed, later on, when Landry had bought a fine farm, which he and his wife managed admirably, she built a comfortable house on their own land where all the poor children of the district came for four hours every weekday, and she and her brother Jeanet took the trouble to teach them, to give them religious instruction, and even to relieve the necessities of those among them who were in want.

She remembered that she had herself been an unfortunate, neglected child, and her own beautiful boys and girls were early taught to be kind and sympathetic toward those who had nobody to pet them and care for them.

But what was Sylvinet doing while all these rejoicings were going on in his family? Something had happened which nobody could understand and which puzzled Father Barbeau very much. About a month after the weddings of his brother and sister, when his father urged him to look around for a wife, he answered that he did not want to marry, but that he had an idea in his head which he wanted to carry out—this was to go and enlist as a soldier. As there are more girls than boys in the families of our country people, and all the hands are needed for the cultivation of the land, it is very seldom that a man volunteers. So this determination of Sylvinet's caused a good deal of surprise, and he assigned no reason for it, except that he had a fancy for a military life, which nobody had ever suspected. He turned a deaf ear to the remonstrances of his father and mother, his sisters and brothers, not even excepting Landry, and they were obliged to appeal to Fanchon, who had better judgment than any member of the family, and whose advice was valuable. She and Sylvinet had a conversation of more than two hours, and when they parted, it was noticed that he and his sister-in-law had both been shedding tears; but they seemed so calm and determined that there were no more objections raised when Sylvinet said that his mind was made up, and Fanchon added that she approved his resolution and thought it would turn out to be the best thing for him in the end. As it seemed probable that she knew more about the matter than she chose to tell, no one ventured to offer any opposition, and even Mother Barbeau gave in, though she shed a good many tears over it. Landry was in despair, but his wife said, "It is God's will and our duty to let Sylvain go. Believe me, I know what I am talking about, and ask no more questions."

Landry accompanied his brother as far as he could on his journey. He had insisted on carrying Sylvain's bundle on his shoulder, and when he handed it to him, it seemed as if he were tearing the heart out of his body. He went home to his dear wife, who nursed him tenderly, for he was really ill with grief for a whole month.

Sylvain did not fall ill, but pursued his way to the frontier; for it was in the times of the great and glorious wars of Napoleon. Though he had never had the least liking for the army, he kept his inclinations under such control that he soon gained the reputation of being a good soldier, brave in action, like a man who attaches no value to his life, and yet as amenable to discipline as a child, and living with all the austerity and rigorous simplicity of the ancients. As he had a very fair education, he soon won his promotion, and after ten years of gallant service and many hardships, he was promoted to captain and was also decorated with the Cross of the Legion of Honor.

"Oh, if he would only come home after all these years," said

Mother Barbeau to her husband, the evening of the day on which they had received a delightful letter from him, filled with kind messages for everybody; for Landry, for Fanchon, and indeed for the whole family, old and young. "Here he is, almost a general, and it is time he had a rest."

"He has rank enough without exaggerating it," said Father Barbeau, "and it is a great honour for a peasant's family."

"Fadette predicted it," said Mother Barbeau. "Yes, indeed, she told us long ago how it would turn out."

"All the same," said the father, "I shall never understand how it was that his tastes turned so suddenly in that direction, and how his disposition changed so completely—he who was so quiet and so fond of his ease."

"Old man, our daughter-in-law knows a good deal more about that than she will tell, but it is not easy to deceive so fond a mother as I am, and I think I know as much about it as our Fadette."

"I think that it is about time you told me."

"Well," said Mother Barbeau, "our Fanchon is too powerful an enchantress, and she exerted more influence over Sylvinet than she intended. When she saw how the charm was working, she would gladly have dispelled it, or done something to diminish its force, but she could not, and our Sylvinet, seeing that he was becoming too fond of his brother's wife, went away from a sense of honour, in which he was sustained and encouraged by Fanchon."

"If that is the case," said Father Barbeau, scratching his ear, "I fear that he will never marry, for the nurse of Clavières said long ago that his infatuation for his brother would cease should he ever fall in love, but that his heart was too tender and passionate ever to love more than once."

CPSIA information can be obtained
at www.ICGtesting.com
Printed in the USA
LVHW022346041222
734572LV00003B/362